Slaughter City

Poet and playwright Naomi Wallace is from Kentucky. Her first play, *The War Boys*, staged at the Finborough Theatre, London, in 1993, won Wallace 'exceptional acclaim for the daring way she stormed traditional male preserves by writing about a wholly male experience' (*Time Out*). *In the Heart of America*, an erotic and disturbing drama set during the Gulf War, was first produced at the Bush Theatre, London, and was winner of the Susan Smith Blackburn Award in 1995: 'It has the vigour and mystical overtones of raw Sam Shepard and the grace and sensuality of a poet' (*Guardian*). *One Flea Spare*, Bush Theatre, London, October 1995, confirmed her early promise: 'Marvellously comic . . . Thrillingly original . . . Impeccable and deeply moving . . . Exquisitely memorable' (*The Times*).

by the same author

ONE FLEA SPARE
(in *Bush Theatre Plays*)

NAOMI WALLACE

Slaughter City

faber and faber
LONDON · BOSTON

To my father Henry F. Wallace – the Rose Island Red

First published in 1996
by Faber and Faber Limited
3 Queen Square London WC1N 3AU

Photoset by Parker Typesetting Service, Leicester
Printed in England by Clays Ltd, St Ives plc

A CIP record for this book
is available from the British Library

ISBN 0-571-17812-X

2 4 6 8 10 9 7 5 3 1

I came to the cities in a time of disorder
When hunger ruled.
I came among men in a time of uprising
And I revolted with them.
So the time passed away
Which on earth was given me.

I ate my food between massacres.
The shadow of murder lay upon my sleep.
And when I loved, I loved with indifference.
I looked upon nature with impatience.
So the time passed away
Which on earth was given me.

In my time streets led to the quicksand.
Speech betrayed me to the slaughterer.
There was little I could do. But without me
The rulers would have been more secure. This was my hope.

'To Those Born Later', Bertolt Brecht

Foreword

'*I was boxing and weighing thirty-pound boxes of neck bones and pig tails and my back started going bad so they put me up on the third floor in the restrooms, sweeping and mopping. I developed nerve compression in my shoulder, and I'd hurt my neck prior to that. At one point I couldn't even raise my arm past elbow level. The doctor put me on all these restrictions. No repetitive lifting over ten to fifteen pounds. No pushing, pulling, groping or squeezing. And so the safety director there at Fischer told me that they didn't have anything else for me to do.*'

I had phoned Wanda Maloney – the speaker above and a former worker at Fischer Packing Company – to gain more 'material' for *Slaughter City*. Although I felt uneasy in my role as some sort of cultural anthropologist, passing through lives and circumstances alien to my own, as our conversation continued (Wanda patiently describing for me the contents of different contracts and the details of her medical history) it was clear that Wanda and workers like her could not only provide theatre with material but also with a language and liveliness that we might learn from and that demands to be heard:

'*I'm 53 years old. I've got no disability, no compensation. No insurance. Nothing. I've got nothing. I worked hard for them. I gave them everything I had as far as my body being able to work. I've done jobs that women didn't do like pushing tubs that weighed 2–3,000 pounds. I really, really put my heart into my work and then after I get something wrong with me they just throw me out to the dogs. In my wildest dreams I never thought it would happen like this. I wasn't a trouble-maker. I'd never even been called to the office! Somewhere there has to be protection for people like me. But where is it?'*

That same hot Kentucky August week of 1992 when I spoke with Wanda, I found myself standing outside a small brick building off of Dixie Highway, on the outskirts of Louisville. This was the union building of Local 227 of the United Food and Commercial Workers which had been out on strike against the Fischer Packing Company for months now and had only recently gone back to work without a contract due to the management's threat to permanently replace them. I had called ahead and made an appointment with Chad Young, an organizer sent down from the International to work with the Local. I told him I was writing a play on workers in the meat industry and that I wanted to talk about the background to the recent strike and the conditions of their work, etc. Chad gave some thought to the etceteras I might need for my writing to be credible so that when I arrived he had in the office with him seven Fischer workers (some of whom would not be rehired later due to their union activity) who were willing to speak with me about their side of the story. At one point I asked if any of them had been injured on the job. All of them had. A couple of them rolled up their sleeves or lifted their shirts to show me where they had been cut by knives or burned by chemicals. Three others displayed their hands, disfigured and swollen with arthritis (most workers in the industry have arthritis, due to the constant change in temperatures within the building). Others were on their second or third operation for carpal tunnel syndrome (a repetitive motion disease). One man had his arm in a sling. As one worker, Artie Koch, put it: 'When you're sent into war, you ought to get hazardous duty pay.' These workers weren't getting that kind of pay. Their salaries had been dropping steadily for ten years now.

In both Britain and the United States there has been a systematic rollback of workers' rights and the rights of unions. Margaret Thatcher's victory against the miners' strike and Ronald Reagan's firing of the air-traffic controllers signalled the wanton deregulation of laws that protected workers and their rights (as well as a *regularizing* of the rule of multinational corporations). Simultaneously, the attrition of the culture and history of labour was stepped up; a consciousness of labour struggle and the validity of unions in mainstream culture plummeted to record lows. In other words, the last decade or so has seen the accelerated repression and distortion of the lives of the majority. Workers are working longer for less, and illegal firings have gone up six-fold. Both countries have the lowest wages in the industrial world. Anti-unionism flourishes, working conditions further deteriorate and inhumane (and global) 'restructuring' abounds. In the USA alone, 6,000 workers die on the job each year – close to 20 a day.* And certainly in the USA, the destruction of unions has been the main factor in the decline of safety regulations as well as real wages. Corporate profits, on the other hand, have, in the USA, reached all-time highs.

Down at Local 227, I asked the questions and the Fischer's workers gave the answers, which I recorded on tape. Then I just shut up and listened as they talked among themselves, about their work, about the food drive, about a worrying violent incident near the picket-line that they

*As the newsletter *CounterPunch* recently detailed: since 1970 'Over 200,000 American workers have lost their lives through the quarter century; nearly two million have been permanently disabled and well over two million workers died from disease incurred from workplace conditions. In the same period only a handful of employers have been prosecuted and just one . . . sent to jail (for 45 days)' (*CounterPunch*, Vol. 2, No. 21). The Republicans, with little hindrance from the Clinton administration, seek to further gut the Occupational Safety and Health Administration, whose job it is to protect workers.

say was prompted by a Fischer security guard. And the more I listened the more I realized just how fiercely the languages of labour have been repressed, and how many of us with presumptions towards a more democratic society don't even know what it is that we are no longer hearing:

'I was working a split-double and I was running the boilers in the morning and I was coming back on third shift to run temperatures. We'd been talking about changing these gauges on the number two hog box for at least a month and I went back there and changed these pressure gauges on this ammonia line. Each unit is five units and the first two broke loose real nice and I changed them and the third one I get to, it breaks. I got ninety pounds of pressurized ammonia shootin' straight up in my face and I get second-degree burns all over my face, my neck and inside my mouth. I go to first aid and no one knows anything about it but me. So I'm slinging junk and shit off my face and yelling for someone to stop that leak. And then I pass out. When I wake up, there's three supervisors floatin' over my head, trying to make out that I'm the one who fucked up. Shit, ninety percent of those lines in there are just accidents waiting to happen.'

Rendered visible through this voice are the immediate and stark power relations of capitalism. These are rarely recognized or allowed to be seen. No burns were evident on Gus Lazrouitch's face. To my blank gaze he answered:

'Second-degree burns. That's why you can't tell. That ammonia is so cold in a liquid form and it touches you and it's like taking a lit match–tttssshhh–it will burn you that quick. That's what it does in a vapour form in your lungs. I don't produce regular tears anymore. I cry dry.'

If, as Marx so eloquently put it, 'Capital comes dripping from head to foot, from every pore, with blood and dirt,' those that work in the blood and the dirt have stories, have histories which not only help us understand the machinations of capital but also provide us with examples of the humanity, the dignity and the outrage capital seeks to deny.

It is due to the grace and grit, intelligence and humour of the workers of both Local 227 of the UFCW in Louisville, Kentucky, and the locked-out workers of Local 7837 of the UPIU at the Staley plant (a highly profitable subsidiary of the British multinational giant, Tate & Lyle, makers of Domino sugar) in Decatur, Illinois, that *Slaughter City* has come into being. Without their generosity in sharing both their despair and relentless hope, this play would not have happened.

Naomi Wallace
December 1995

Characters

Roach, an African American worker in her mid-thirties
Maggot, a white worker in her mid-thirties
Bandon, a white worker in his early twenties
Cod, a white worker of Irish descent, mid-thirties
Tuck, an African American, mid-forties
Textile Worker, a woman in her twenties
Sausage Man, a white man, somewhat elderly, energetic
Mr Baquin, a white company manager in his fifties

Time: Now and then.
Place: Slaughter City, USA.
Set: Minimal and not 'realistic'.

Slaughter City was first performed by the Royal
Shakespeare Company at the Pit, Barbican Centre,
London, on 17 January 1996 with the following cast:

Textile Worker Mairead Carty
Roach Lisa Gaye Dixon
Cod Olwen Fouere
Maggot Sophie Stanton
Brandon Alexis Daniel
Mr Baquin Linal Haft
Sausage Man Robert Langdon Lloyd
Tuck Rudolph Walker

Directed by Ron Daniels
Designed by Ashley Martin-Davis

Act One

The stage is empty but for a woman **Textile Worker**, *her back to us, working hunched over her cloth. She speaks as if in a trance.* **Cod** *is elsewhere on stage, watching her work. We are in a textile factory setting, 'somewhere' in the past.*

Textile Worker
Pull the cloth, punch it down, cut three out and trace.
Hurry, hurry, don't slow down, keep your cheer and grace.

Cod Could you look up for a second? Hey.

Textile Worker
Pull the cloth, punch it down, cut three out and trace.

Cod (*calls*) Is anybody out there?

Textile Worker
Hurry, hurry, don't slow down, keep your cheer and grace.

Cod The doors are locked. (*to Textile Worker*) I'm talking to you.

Textile Worker When I daydream, my hands sweep the cloth –

Cod What floor are we on?

Textile Worker – like water over the keys of a piano.

We hear the distorted sound of a siren in the distance.

Cod We've got to get out of here.

Textile Worker (*touching his face gently*) Oh what eyes you have. Black eyes. Like my eyes.

I

Cod I haven't got any eyes. I'm not even born yet.

The woman turns back to her cloth to work. Transfixed, Cod watches her.

SCENE ONE

Lights up on **Maggot, Roach** *and* **Brandon** *working. They are hosing down the heads of carcasses which are suspended above them and slicing off bits of gristle from the bone. When the workers work, the feeling should be one of the intensity of industrial labour here on earth and perhaps also in hell.*

Roach Maggot?

No answer.

Maggot? Come on, sweetie. I said I was sorry. It was just a joke, wasn't it, Brandon?

Brandon A masterstroke, an okeydoke joke.

Maggot A just plain you haven't-got-any-brains-for-God-left-to-suck-out-of-your-skull joke.

Roach Did you eat it?

Brandon Didn't even pause 'til she got to the claws.

Roach Maggot? Come on.

Maggot Not unless you buy me three packs of brand-name smokes and on third shift you snap guts and let me scale.

Roach You know I won't snap guts.

Maggot I've been snappin' guts since I was seventeen.

Brandon Princess of Excrementis.

Maggot Just because I turned you down for a Dairy Queen date three years ago . . .

Brandon That was before I realized that what you need is a dull blade, baby, a blade that won't cut meat.

Double bell sounds, which means a short break for the workers. At the moment the horn sounds, all work/ assembly line movement stops. Maggot flexes her hands, which are hurting her.

Roach Two packs of generics and I'll go third shift on the night you want off, 'cept Saturday –

Brandon (*interrupts*) Hey! Here it comes: I'm startin' to itch.

Cod enters, headed for the kill floor. He is a slim young Irishman, who is stronger than he looks. Brandon jumps in front of Cod and pretends to sword fight.

Unsheathe from your scabbard, you scoundrel, you fleabane, you scabrous snake.

Cod does not respond.

Look at this ladies. Not a peep. Why, they're no fun, these bacterial spots. And Lord how they –

Maggot and Roach Itch, itch, itch.

Brandon (*like a commercial*) Are you covered with raised, roughened or unwholesome patches?

Maggot and Roach Scratch, scratch, scratch.

Brandon Do you sometimes feel a little down, like a crust of hard blood and serum over a wound?

The three workers circle Cod.

Maggot and Roach (*together*) Are you characterized by crustaceous spots?

Brandon Then you need Local 226.

Maggot Only Local 226 –

Roach, Maggot and Brandon Don't need you. (*They stand in a circle around Cod.*)

Roach You know what scab stands for?

Maggot, Brandon and Roach Stupid Cunts And Bastards.

Cod spits on the ground at their feet.

Roach (*speaks*) It's raining, it's pouring –

Maggot and Roach (*together*) The scab's gone a-whoring!

Maggot Watch you don't bump your head.

Brandon Or you won't be back in the morning!

Maggot begins to steal her knife, the others do the same. Roach hums a tune and then the three workers sing the following. When one of them sings, the others hum.

Brandon
I'm gonna cut you, Scabby, gonna cut you deep
With my sweet, blue kisses, gonna send you off to sleep.

Maggot
I'm gonna slice you, sweet heart, gonna slice you wide –

Roach
With my hot fast lips I'm gonna take you for a ride.

Bell sounds again. The workers move back to their jobs. Cod stands silently, watching them.

SCENE TWO

Mr Baquin *in his office, with* **Tuck,** *a supervisor.*

Tuck Mood. The mood?

4

Baquin Yes. What's the mooood in the packhouse?

Tuck Sickly. Yeah, a sickly mood in there.

Baquin Well, their boycott of our products has put a dent in our sales, but a dent is a dent. We can survive a dent. What we need is a mooooove. (*Clears his throat.*) A turn in the right direction. Some better weather. What do you say we . . . What's your name again?

Tuck Tuck. Supervisor Tuck.

Baquin Yes, well, fellows come and go here. Mostly Affirmative Action types. They don't always last –

Tuck (*interrupts*) Affirmative action didn't get this job for me.

Baquin I didn't mean to imply. No. Not you. But then, why you? What makes Buck special?

Tuck I started on the kill floor, sir. About fifteen years ago. I worked my way up. Now I take night classes at Bellarmin. Just about got my degree.

Baquin Where do you see yourself in five years?

Tuck Do you like your job?

Baquin Clever! Very clever.

Tuck Yeah. But I've also been cut. (*He shows his arm.*) Sliced. (*He shows his torso.*) And hacked. (*He shows where a finger is maimed.*)

Baquin That's, that's very convincing. So what do you say we up the pace again? It's either that or we close down and reopen on the other side of the map, cut wages in half and let her rip.

Tuck Some families have been around since we opened fifty years ago. You can't replace that kind of labour.

Baquin Don't get sentimental. We've got a business to run. Special interests are slicing our hearts, gutting innovation, shredding our ability to compete –

Tuck You've got two Mercedes.

Baquin That's what I mean. Fellow that runs IBP's got three.

Tuck They won't go easy for the mechanical sharpener, and seniority rights are still top of the list.

Baquin Seniority rights. I need capable workers. A worker is like a nose. It runs good, runs on time. But like all things, it get's stuffed. You pick it. It gets stuffed again. It starts costing too much to pick. What do you expect me to do? Be their grandmother and carry out their snot rags in their old age?

Tuck I would get rid of some trouble-makers.

Baquin I've done that.

Tuck There are some more.

Baquin Tell me something, son. I heard a rumour the other day that some of our boys in the packhouse aren't circumcized. The Board doesn't like it. It's not good for packhouse reputation. (*Beat.*) What about you?

   No answer from Tuck.

Well, if you're not, you should go get it done. Those little hats collect dirt. And you don't seem like the kind of man to collect dirt.

Tuck No . . .

Baquin What we need is to raise the spirits around here. We need to give the union the feeling that it has a voice. That the boss listens. That we're a team.

Tuck They want a new contract and a guaranteed pace.

Baquin That's not a team concept. Let's start a reading circle. Management will supply the books. We'll discuss literature. Start with Thomas Hardy. (*Beat*) What about an environmental programme? We could get a committee together to discuss Partula Affinis. (*He holds up a glass bowl.*) It's the only current member of a small and exclusive club of species that has been wiped out by man.

Tuck What is it?

Baquin A snail.

Tuck Looks like snot.

Baquin It's the last single snail of its kind. I bought it from the University of Virginia. Under the table deal. They get our sliced meats 30 per cent off. It's a hermaphrodite, this one. If it wants to, it can mate with itself. When this small mollusc dies, its species will enter the eternal night of extinction. Hard to imagine, isn't it? (*Beat.*) Do you think we could stir up some interest? An after-work hobby?

Tuck They're pretty tired when they get off work.

Baquin Imagine. The ultimate loneliness. To be the last of your kind. (*Beat.*) Who's that kid, the one always sparking trouble over the knives? College kid. Full of spunk.

Tuck Brandon.

Baquin Find a reason to fire him.

Tuck He's one of our best with a knife.

Baquin Then promote him. That should turn him around.

Tuck By the way, he's back. The guy with the sausage grinder, old hand-held thing. Nasty. He's waiting in the hall to see you. He won't leave. Says he started the company.

Baquin Nonsense. No one started this company. It's been here since . . . the beginning of time. (*Beat.*) Now, give me a check on their . . . on their . . . mooooood again. (*Clears his throat.*) At the end of the week.

Tuck I'll do that, Mr Baquin.

Baquin Thataboy, Buck.

Tuck exits. Baquin sits at his desk and clears his throat again and speaks aloud, though he is alone.

At the end of the week. Give me a report on their . . . (*He looks around him, in some distress. He tries again.*)At the end of the week. Give me a report on their . . . general well-being.

SCENE THREE

Brandon is showing Roach how to pull loins, one of the toughest jobs in the industry.

Brandon Reach and pull. Reach and pull. Got it? (*Beat.*) Half the men I know can't pull loins.

Roach For a number one pay bracket for a whole week, I'm damn sure gonna try.

Brandon Now you got seven to nine coming at you a minute. When the horn goes for the speed up, you get up to twelve.

He puts his hands on hers to show her. She pulls away.

Roach Just show me, OK?

Brandon The important thing is you've got to dip your knife before each cut. Like this. And swing the blade out over the loin like this. You have to be quick. Real quick.

8

Roach I got it.

They pull loins side by side.

Brandon You've got . . . nice, quick arms.

Roach Why don't you go on back to college, where you belong?

Brandon 'Cause I like the pay.

Roach That's the difference between you and me, besides the colour: you like the pay. I need it.

Brandon When I started working here, I vomited every Monday morning. They dropped me down on the kill floor pulling black guts and cleaning chitterlings. Hog shit in my nose, in my mouth, all day long. Then I was trimming jaw bones. Lost a thumb, see? Moving up. Moving up in the pay bracket. Ten cents more. Fifteen cents more. All the time waiting to get to the knives. Then I was head boner. Slipped a disk twice. Twenty-five cents more. Then moving up again to a scalder. Forty cents. Then forty-five. Hot. That was too damn hot. Then I was bung dropper. Too fucking intimate, cutting the assholes out of hogs. One guy slipped his bung and cut my left thigh to the bone. Then I was splitter. Top rate bracket. Bingo. New used car. Two-bedroom apartment, one for me, one for my television. I like it. I like the money.

Roach You like the money. We're making less now at the top pay bracket than we were at the lowest ten years ago.

Brandon But that's gonna change for me, 'cause I'm moving up to formal combat with the meat, straight into that neat clean seat in the sky.

Roach You don't give a damn about the contract, do you?

Brandon Sure I do. While I'm here. I'm not budging on knife sharpening time. The twenty minutes we got now isn't enough.

Roach It's about more than knives.

Brandon Not to me. What they want is to hire some distempered dildo who doesn't know that one knife is as different from another as two women are different. And this guy is gonna sharpen my knife for me? That fayuousferret will fold that edge over without even knowing it and I'll have to break my back all day long cutting with a dull knife.

Roach Seniority is the priority.

Brandon You never used a loin knife 'til now. Look. The edge of a knife is like a thin piece of hair. What the steel does is it stands it up, so if you angle that steel wrong, you're going to fold the edge over.

Roach Hmmm.

Brandon I was thinking maybe you (*beat*) and me, we could take a stroll. Nothing too fancy, a twirl through the park, a couple of cartwheels 'cross the Belvedere?

Roach I already said no. I'm fifteen years older than you.

Brandon Maybe you don't dote on white boys.

Roach I don't dote on boys period.

Brandon You're caught up on this colour thing.

Roach Since the day I was born.

Brandon Well, get over it, Roach. Cast it behind you.

Roach Just scale it off me like a fish. Right. Why are you here? Why don't you toddle on back to the U and get some more of that financial aid. Though I doubt you'll learn to figure this side of the fence even if you sit bare-assed on the barbed wire.

Brandon Light the candles. It's gonna be another pity party! And guess who gets the gifts? (*Chants.*)
Cause I'm a little white boy,
And the world's my wind-up toy.
I'm the power of the nation.
I'm source of all creation!

   Double bell sounds for a break. Roach looks at her watch.

Roach Isn't it about time you changed your diapers?

Brandon Every day I wake up and people like you are telling me that the world's a rabbit in my hat, right? That I'm the boss. I can't even get my fuckin' knife sharpened the way I want to. Feel this one they did on the machine.

   He takes her hand to make her feel it. She pulls away.

Roach Don't touch people who don't want to be touched.

Brandon Tell me something. Who got to you first and ruined it for me?

   Calmly, Roach slaps him.

If you can keep up (*beat*) I'll steel your knife for you.

   Roach doesn't respond.

At least until you get the hang of it.

Roach And what, Mr Nice Guy, do I have to do in return?

Brandon Like ice cream?

Roach Depends.

Brandon On what?

Roach On the cone.

Brandon When I said I liked . . . It wasn't a line. Your arms. They're (*beat*) stalwart and sturdy.

11

Roach They get the job done.

Brandon I like to eat mine out of a cup.

SCENE FOUR

Supervisor Tuck stands watching Cod sweep offal down the drain holes.

Tuck It's an odd name. Know what it means?

Cod No.

Tuck Look it up. I did. It's a fish. From the cold North Atlantic. (*Beat.*) Not too bad here, is it? Though I never liked hogs myself. Small eyes.

Cod That transfer you mentioned? I'd rather stay in one place.

Tuck In Latin your name is *Gadus morrhua*. Don't you think Gadus has just a bit more status to it? And status might be what a guy like you needs, Gadus. Gadus?

Cod Yeah.

Tuck You missed a bit. To your left. (*Beat.*) Did you know you were once thought of as a nigger, Gadus? Now don't take offence. I know white folks don't like being called nigger. It gets them confused. (*Beat.*) Why are you making those puny strokes. Watch me.

> *Tuck takes the broom and makes some masterful and fancy sweeps with it.*

History, Gadus. You ever read? That's where you'll find the key.

> *Tuck gives Cod back the broom.*

When you Irishmen came over here in the 1800s, after that

12

British potato problem, you were called a dark race, low-browed and savage. Oh yeah. You were more feared than us blacks. You were the Celtic Beast and you chased the women and raped the chickens. That's a fact. You lived side by side with us in the slums. Chums we were, you and me. Chummed up and slumming it together. Then you were given a raise. That raise was the right to call us nigger and the right not to be called a nigger yourself. So you see, whiteness don't have to be a colour, Gadus. It can be a wage. (*Watching him sweep.*) That's it. Use your shoulders. Pull and push. Pull and push.

Cod The kill floor. I like it there.

Tuck We'll see. We need you where we need you. (*Beat.*) Hold your head up. Don't stoop. A man like you shouldn't stoop. Gadus?

Cod It's just that you're standing on the drain and I can't get to it.

Tuck doesn't move.

Tuck Do you dream, Gadus? I dream. But a dream is like the waves a fly makes struggling on the surface of the water. When the fly stops struggling, so does the dream. (*Beat.*) Gadus? You're all wet.

Cod It's the heat, sir.

Tuck It's only seventy in here.

Cod It's hotter than that.

Tuck Push and pull, Gadus. Push and pull.

SCENE FIVE

Maggot and Roach are trimming ham bones.

13

Roach A scab's a scab.

Maggot That doesn't mean he don't have a cute ass.

Roach It's scab ass, honey. And that sort of ass never changes its spots. You just like the underdogs. You ever been with someone with a nice coloured ass?

Maggot I was with a French guy once.

Roach French is white. (*Beat.*) A lot of scabs they brought in here were black. When we said we'd come back to our jobs without a contract, they fired most of those scabs. Pieces of meat. Black pieces of meat. (*Beat.*) I see our boys with their Local 226 T-shirts on and they are calling them scabs everything they can think of but racial. 'Cause it's not allowed. 'Cause we are above that. But I can hear that word behind our white boys' teeth: (*whispers*) nigger. Nigger. (*Beat.*) That word ever get stuck up behind your teeth, Maggot? When you're cursin' and yellin' at those scabs and you're madder than hell, you ever feel that word on your tongue?

Maggot How long have we been best friends, Roach?

Roach If promotion time comes, who are they gonna promote, you or me?

Maggot Neither of us is gonna get promoted.

Roach But if they do, are you gonna tell them I been here three years longer than you, that I got seniority, or are you just gonna grab it?

A light flashes. This signals a speed up. We see the workers work faster.

They're not supposed to speed up 'til after lunch.

Maggot You ever done it with a white man?

Roach How white are we talking?

Maggot Ice white.

Roach I'm going up to Green River this weekend.

Maggot You won't sleep with a man because he's white?!

Roach I got a new set of spinners, yellow tails. Want to come?

Maggot Got no money for gas.

Roach Shhh. Look who's coming for supper.

Cod enters with huge meat hooks and chains. He wipes them down and stacks/hangs them.

Aren't you in the smoke department this week?

Cod Injecto pump's down.

Maggot You look like a nice young man. Where did you find it in that puny little soul of yours to cross our picket line when we were out on strike? Give me a straight answer.

The following dialogue is fired back and forth rapidly.

Cod I have kids to feed.

Maggot Not with our jobs.

Cod It's not your job if you're out there.

Maggot All they want to do is use you like a piece of meat.

Cod Where you gonna work where they aren't gonna treat you like a piece of meat?

Roach Come back on that one, Maggot. We need a comeback.

Maggot is silent.

Two points for the scab!

Cod You two talk this bold to the company?

Maggot We haven't got a new contract 'cause low-lifes like you crossed the picket line.

Cod I haven't got any kids.

Roach Always sounds better when you bring in the kids.

Cod I want to join your local.

Maggot You can't join a local once you cross their pickets.

Roach Trying to change his spots.

Cod A man can have a change of heart, can't he?

Roach You're no man, Spotty, and you'll never be part of this union.

Cod I used to be union. A miner. Long time ago . . . Harlen County . . . Kentucky . . . No . . . It was the Colorado coal strike. Dug our own graves underground. Day by day. Ate coal, pissed coal, shat coal. Then one day, doesn't matter which day, you just couldn't dig anymore and you lay down in the grave you dug and died. After years of it, we went out on strike. Just said 'No'. We figured that would change something. Well it did. Rockefeller called out the National Guard. They came down on the Ludlow colony, burned our tents and opened fire. Sixty-six of us dead.

Roach When did this happen?

Cod I was a telephone linesman. I went through the wreck the next day and lifted an iron cot that was covering a pit. There were bodies inside. Burned the way meat gets burned and goes black and small.

Roach Now wait a minute.

Cod Eleven children and two women.

Maggot You said you were a miner.

Cod Smoke rising off their bodies like light.

Roach So how come you were a telephone linesman?

Cod After the massacre, workers came from all over the country, brought sticks and guns, whatever they could find. The President sent in the Federal Troops to restore order.

Roach This is bullshit.

Cod He restored it alright. The miners went back to the mines for less than they came out. Not one militiaman or mine guard was ever indicted for the killings.

Roach We didn't hear about any killings.

Maggot People don't get shot on strike.

Cod Who's talking people? I'm talking miners.

Maggot Fuck you.

Bell sounds for break. All movement stops.

Cod Do you know what it's like to die in a fire?

Maggot This guy's great. I want to marry this guy.

Roach Fabulous idea. Come on over here, Maggot. Let me dress you up. (*She picks up strips of bacon.*) I'll make your veil.

Roach hangs strips of bacon across Maggot's hair and face so they form a kind of meat veil. Maggot hums the wedding song.

Doesn't she look wonderful. Mr I-can-tell-two-bitches-anything-I-like-and-they'll-believe-me? Now, side by side. But how shall we dress the groom? Maggot, help me. (*Beat.*) I've got an idea. (*She runs for a bucket of scraps and blood.*)

Maggot Nice thinking.

*The women dip their hands in it and begin to paint Cod
with it. He submits. Roach paints cheeks on his face
with the blood.*

Roach Rosy cheeks for you.

Maggot slicks his hair back with the slop.

Maggot Oh the hair is beginning to shine.

Cod I could make a difference. I've been around.

Maggot No, no. You're getting married.

Cod I like you. If I didn't, I'd break your neck.

Maggot What a big mouth you have, Granny.

*Maggot kisses Cod on the mouth. He doesn't respond.
She kisses him again. This time he responds and pushes
her violently and then throws her into Roach. Both of
the women realize the game has gone too far.*

Cod I didn't choose this place. You understand that? It
chose me.

*Cod approaches Maggot and gently pulls the raw bacon
slices from her hair as he speaks.*

You know the guy whose job I took stands outside the
packhouse, all day, uptight, calls me a meat-fucking-scab.
At 5 a.m. when I walk in, I look the other way. I grew up
in the cities, never touched a hog alive. Here, I touch them
in pieces. I stroke them from the inside out, where they're
wet; it's not right. Once I slipped on some guts, took a dive
with my face in it. I could swear the bloody slab made a
sound, a sneer, like glass dragging on glass. (*Beat.*) The
man whose job I took, each day, he spits at me on my way

18

in. He misses. He spits again on my way out. He misses again. If I could risk this job, I'd ask him if he's heard it, like I did, the meat, talking to him or when his nose is full of blood and his hair webbed with fat, if he's ever heard it laugh. (*Moves away from the women.*) We're all shit without money. The company rolls the coin to the centre of the strike and we have no choice but to kill for it. Once that guy spit at me and got me right on the brow. But I still wouldn't look him in the face. I just walked into the packhouse. If meat laughs, I'd like to tell him, it's because it's no longer an animal, but flesh turned the wrong way, turned inside out, like I am, like we all are now.

The women watch him in silence.

SCENE SIX

The packhouse is dark and empty. We see a figure wandering alone and carefully looking over the packhouse. He is turning what looks like a small musical organ but it's a hand grinder for sausages that is hung about his neck. He speaks to the space around him.

Sausage Man I came across the ocean, from Zweibrucken, in the late 1800s. I ground meat in my own back yard. I didn't have a pot to piss in. Sausages. I made sausages. All the little bits of bone and gut and cartilage that the rest of the world threw away, I made into something useful. Something edible. And I wrote the song. The sausage song. I wrote the lullaby that rocked this city to sleep. (*Sings.*)

Fischers, the Sausage Makin' people
Makes it fun to be hungry.

With my two hands I created an empire out of a single sausage. And I fed you. I fed you! And what do I get in return? No one is happy making my sausages anymore.

But still I grind and grind. I fill the skins with meat. I make it fun to be hungry. (*He grinds his grinder faster.*) Ah, what a sound. The sound of hundreds, thousands of sausages filling up the empty spaces in the world. Sausages filling up the empty spaces in our very souls. I love that sound. Like the world in my hands. Like the world going to pieces in my hands.

SCENE SEVEN

Brandon, Roach and Maggot working at metal tables.

Brandon I don't trust him. He's fractious.

Maggot The man's got passion.

Roach Only for himself.

Maggot If we strike again, he'll join us.

Roach If we strike again, the replacements will turn their backs.

Brandon (*to Maggot*) You really want to stick your neck out for this yokel?

Roach He won't be a part of my union. What's left of it.

Maggot You're a tight ass, Roach.

Roach Yeah? He's a scab and you're an itch and if you two get to scratching someone is gonna bleed.

Maggot You wouldn't know an itch if it crawled up your leg and bit you.

Roach An itch is something a dog gets.

> *Maggot barks like a dog, then she picks up a piece of meat and takes a bite out of it.*

You white girls are disgusting. You take a joke so far it'll kill you.

Brandon (*to Roach, to interrupt the women*) So . . . when are you gonna succumb to my sugar cone, baby?

Roach You're making me nauseous.

Brandon 'I find my heart inside my ribs aroused by your impertinence.'

Maggot Brandon.

Brandon Homer.

Maggot Give it up.

Brandon (*to Roach*) Come on, darlin', I'm hankering. I'm baffled and balked. Just give me half a wink.

Roach What a charmer!

Maggot Could charm the shit out of a dead rabbit's ass.

Brandon Not much up top, Maggot, and less down below. For a fruit tramp baby, you're a seedy specimen.

Maggot Listen, little man. You don't, can't, won't ever get me hot 'cause I got a clit the size of a small rodent and I'd just snap you in half like a corn-nut.

Roach (*to Brandon*) If we vote on letting him join, will you back me up with a negative?

Brandon I'll back up, bend down and roll up just as far as you want me to. Well?

Roach I'll go for a coke with you, Brandon. A coke. For an hour.

Maggot Look who's using the itch.

Roach But I'm not gonna let you watch me sip it.

Brandon Why not? I want to see you sip it. I want to watch that liquid ascend through the straw, up into your moist and marvellous . . . Fuck! (*He's cut himself on his knife.*) Look at that! Look at that, God damn it. Just try it, he says. Just try it. Machine gives it a good edge. Fuck his edge. (*Shouts to someone off-stage.*) Fuck your edge. (*Beat.*) They're going to replace us. Then they won't need the top rate knife boys. The mechanical will do it.

Roach You better check that at the clinic.

The bell sounds for a break.

Brandon And a mechanical won't ask for a raise. Well, we'll see about that. (*Shouts to off-stage.*) We'll see about that! One more time and you won't have any knives left to steel. (*He is furious now and drops to his knees and begins hacking at the floor until the knife is ruined. He throws it aside. Silence. Then he speaks quietly.*) That'll fuck your edge.

Cod staggers in. He takes centre stage. He shouts.

Cod I been robbed!

The workers make various exclamations of 'What happened?' and 'Tell us?' Brandon wraps a makeshift bandage around his hand.

I been robbed! By the capitalist system!

Maggot Jesus Christ!

Roach Moron!

Brandon Fuck off!

They ignore him and relax on their 'break'. Cod continues with his 'show'. Cod climbs up on a higher level to 'soap box' them.

Cod What we need around here is some direct action.

Shall I tell you what direct action means? The worker on the job shall tell the boss when and where the worker shall work, how long and for what wages and under what conditions.

They ignore him.

The working class and the employer class have nothing in common?

They don't respond.

IWW? Industrial Workers of the World? OK. How many of you don't have arthritis from workin' the cold and wet? Maggot? You've got carpal tunnel in both hands.

Maggot Been operated on twice.

Cod Roach? Back so bad from lifting you got to roll out of bed in the morning?

Roach Why do you think we went on strike to begin with?

Cod How about you, Brandon? So tired after a split-double, chasin' half-crazed steers at midnight you just can't get that erection you need for Saturday night?

Brandon Fuck your dog, your cat and any other carnivorous animals you own.

Cod Fucking? Well. Yes. Now fucking is the key, no matter with who or where or how, and each time a worker comes in this world, the possibility for their taking power increases, just a little.

Maggot Oh, Scabby's talking dirty!

Cod Because coming is the body's way of saying fuck you to the rules and regulations.

Brandon Fuck you.

Cod (*continuing*) It's catching! Fuck you to the bowing and scraping we live by just to eat, fuck you to the poverty, to the dismemberment of our souls, day after day, hour after hour. When a worker comes, when we come, it's our body's way of saying: 'I am radiant and I am fearless and I will not be disposed of. I am not a piece of meat.'

Cod has got their attention now.

Whatever we win or lose here is what meat workers will have to accept all over the country, at Swift, Armour, IBP, Hormel.

Roach Scrambles over the top of us to get at our jobs.

Brandon Pisses on our backs on his way in.

Roach And now he's talking about thinking big, talking about greater good.

Cod Things aren't always what they seem.

Maggot Down here they are.

Cod I'm not the enemy.

Brandon Oh no? I saw you usin' a blade the other day that some kid sharpened for you on the mechanical. I didn't hear a peep of protest out of you.

Roach Just big hot talk.

Maggot Shit. (*Her hand isn't working for her anymore. In anger she begins to bang her numb hand against the work table.*) Wake up, damn you. Wake up!

Cod (*sings*)
If there's a hell it's as hot as this
Standing all day in the blood and piss.

Maggot I'll cut you off!

Cod (*sings*)
We work in the war zone and the wages we pull
Aren't enough to keep a dog's tit full.

SCENE EIGHT

*Brandon alone after everyone has gone home. A
makeshift, bloody bandage on his hand, he stands on a
work scaffold, then jumps down and clears the space for
his 'dance'. He places his small cassette player in the
centre of the space and then begins to run, jump and
dance around the stage. The feeling is one of a body
taking complete control over the space around it. There
is a part of a wrapped carcass hanging from the ceiling.
Brandon cuts it loose with his knife and it falls. He turns
off the music to begin the second part of his 'show'. He
circles the carcass, then takes off his shirt and speaks. All
this should be stylized. Brandon has done this sort of
'show' before.*

Brandon 'Let sorrow split my heart (*he slashes the
wrapper open to expose the meat*) if ever I did hate thee.'
(*He gently undresses the carcass and speaks to it. Sings.*)
I got a mouth like a spider
And a web for you I'll spin.
Just open up a little wider,
With my spinneret, I'm comin' in.

> *He tries something else for the seduction. Roach is
> watching him from the shadows, unobserved.*

I'll give you the kiss of death, my flower, 'cause I'm the
Triatoma kissing bug, assassin bug, and I'll bite off a hunk
of your heart. (*He throws away the knife and begins to
kiss and nip at the carcass. He then holds up his hands.*)
See the light comin' off my feathers, love? See it? I'm an

angel and I'm gonna reach my wing so far inside you, I'm going to disappear.

He pushes his hand, then his arm, inside the carcass. This should be both sensual and frightening. Roach picks up the knife. She comes up behind him, takes him by the hair and holds the knife to his throat. She is in complete control.

Roach Oh, but that's not enough, my cherub. No. This piece of meat wants your sweet face inside her, your whole head inside her. (*She crushes his face into the carcass, then turns him on his back so she's straddling him, knife still at his throat.*) You like this dream, lover boy? What happens in the end? Does she come like he needs her to, like a train, blasting off, straight up to the sky?

Brandon He'll never know 'cause she doesn't want him.

Roach This is a sad picture if this is how you want me. In case you haven't heard, we don't like to be cut when we come.

Brandon I fuckin' hate you, Roach. I fuckin' hate you 'cause I want you so bad it's like a knife up my ass.

Roach If I could I'd turn it, college boy.

Brandon Tuck is gonna promote me.

Roach Promote you?

Brandon Office work.

Roach You've only been here a couple of years.

Brandon They want me off the kill floor.

Roach Always the fuckin' white boys get promoted.

Brandon I can talk, Roach. Hear how I can talk? I pick up words, all kind of words, big words, small words. I pick up words like a dog picks up fleas. (*Beat.*) But I can't read. How am I going to do office work when I can't read? (*Beat.*) Shit. My face hurts. Damn it.

Roach (*touching his forehead*) You've got a fever.

Brandon Keep your hand there.

Roach You got to get to the hospital. You got blood poisoning.

Brandon You're poisoning me.

Roach Right. Come on. Get up. (*She helps him to his feet.*)

Brandon I'm twenty-two years old. I've never been with a woman.

Roach What are you saying?

Brandon Look at my mouth.

Roach So?

Brandon No. Look at it. The white marks. Like a halo around my mouth.

Roach Pretty.

Brandon When I was fifteen I quit going to school 'cause the words were upside down. Somersaulting. I couldn't keep them in line. I left home and went and lived with my boss. He let me have a corner in his garage. He owned a chain of jewellery stores. I swept, stacked, cooked. One day I dropped a box with some china in it. He hit me until I passed out. When I came to, he was sitting beside me. He had a lure box with him. He said I'd cursed him. I couldn't remember, up 'til then I'd never said a thing but 'Yes, sir'. He said he'd make sure I never spoke against him again. He took some fish line and a hook out of his box and he sewed my mouth shut. That's why I never could kiss a girl.

27

Because it's always bleeding where the line went through. How can you kiss a girl when your mouth is always bleeding?

Roach Your mouth isn't bleeding.

Brandon Yeah it is. I can taste it.

Roach There's no blood on your mouth.

Brandon Every day I can taste it.

SCENE NINE

Baquin and Tuck giving the Sausage Man a tour of the facilities.

Baquin Ah, Baquin's the name, meat's the game. And you are . . .?

Sausage Man I make sausages.

Baquin Ah. Hobby perhaps, or old-style deli? Well, you've come to the right place to see how slaughtering and packing are properly done. (*meaning the packhouse*) So what do you think?

Sausage Man It makes me sad.

Baquin Ah yes. I know. Do you think I haven't spared a thought for the cow, trembling at that final moment, those big brown eyes?

Sausage Man It's not the cows, dear sir.

Baquin Oh, the pigs . . . well, the toys are cute but the real thing . . . Just think of that book about the pigs who take over the farm . . . um . . . Tuck?

Tuck *Animal Farm*, Mr Baquin. Napoleon and –

Baquin (*interrupts*) Right! A great writer, Joyce. If we gave pigs – and I'm sure the cows would be right behind them – if we gave them their declaration of rights . . . Well, who knows, we might all end up as sausages!

Sausage Man The workers, the shop-floor, the union . . .

Baquin They love our sausages!

Sausage Man I'm troubled. Deeply troubled. Too much talk and idleness. Kid-gloves, cowardly tactics. Not how we used to do it. Those times then are here, now. I know the rules. I can say yes, no, stay, go. Open, close and fire! And this company? Ah, if I had ulcers, they'd be the size of oranges by now. Look at you!

Baquin inspects himself.

You're not even triple stitched. I bet you let your socks wear thin before you throw them out!

Tuck Should I get rid of . . .?

Baquin P.R., Tuck. P.R.

Sausage Man What we need is to kindle a spark, ignite a little imagination around here. Have you ever felt your blood boil? It's extraordinary.

Baquin I eat lots of bran. Keeps my stress level under control.

Sausage Man There's too much sympathy nowadays.

Baquin For the cows? The workers? The pigs?

Sausage Man It was different; it used to be an iron-clad operation, lock, stock and barrel. It's a shame.

Baquin (*without a clue*) I know what you mean.

Sausage Man It saddens me.

Baquin I, too, am deeply touched. Nevertheless, I think you're a bit out of date. If you want to start a competitive business, you –

Sausage Man (*interrupts*) Out of date? I'm your future.

Baquin What?

Sausage Man Oh, I'm having no fun at all. Something must be done.

Baquin I agree completely, Mr . . .?

Sausage Man I made the finest sausage links . . .

Baquin (*overlapping so that only 'links' is clearly defined*) Mr Links, you know, it's an age-old conundrum with us in the meat-packing business: where does our sympathy go? I confess, I try to steer clear of those big brown innocent eyes – but man cannot live by greens alone. It thins the blood.

    Sausage Man is leaving. Baquin follows him.

Age old, I confess, yes, and we run a tight ship here and the hands, well, we can't let sympathy out and about or the cows and the pigs, Napolean – right, Tuck? – well, they'd be ruling the roast . . . the roost . . . And be sure to pick up some literature on your way out, we're the professionals.

    Sausage Man is 'gone'.

Ah, the muddled Old School. Never get a business off the ground these days.

SCENE TEN

Cod is soapboxing the workers as they clean up after work. Roach is hosing off her arms and apron, which are covered in blood. Maggot collects offal in a bag. Brandon cleans his knives. He is somewhat crazed with fever.

Cod A spectre is haunting the meat-packing industry. The history of all hitherto –

Roach Hitherto?

Maggot Hitherto?

Cod Of all hitherto existing society is the history of class struggles.

Brandon Do you know there are nine different sorts of pine cones in the world?

Cod Our epoch possesses this distinctive feature –

Brandon How would you like a giant sequoia stuffed up your ass?

Cod – it has simplified the class antagonisms.

Roach Interclass antagonisms: scab versus union.

Cod Society as a whole is more and more splitting up –

Brandon Splitting up. I can do that.

Cod – into two great hostile camps, into two great classes directly facing each other: Bourgeoisie –

Maggot Sounds like imported cheese.

Cod – and Proletariat. (*Sings*)
So fold up your arms and sit where you stand
They're gonna hear us across the land.

Brandon So you like to soap box?

Cod
We're sick of getting nothing but an ear of shit
This time it's enough and we say quit.

Brandon A little exhibition to flaunt your wares?

Cod We have a world to win.

Brandon Could be a world to lose. But since you like to play, let's play. You and me. You believe all it takes is to sing a few words and the boss is going to hand you the plate? All right. Show me some fortitude. Make me afraid.

Cod Sorry about that office job, Brandie. I know you were counting on it.

Brandon Lovely touch. And precise. But let's get back to the matter at hand. Let's say I'm running this packhouse. I'm running this whole joke. (*He tears off his apron and throws it aside.*)

Maggot Sup.'s got two warnings on your file, Brandon.

Brandon And I'm clean. I haven't been standing in blood all day. No gut in my hair. Hands don't shake. My back is straight. Mouth tastes like I just brushed my teeth. Nice. But here you are. Just your average guy, cutting out hog asshole fifteen hours a day, piss running through your veins, gums swimming in steer blood.

Roach Strike three and there won't be nothing the union can do for you anymore.

Brandon No. How about a bitch? Can you play a bitch? I bet you can. And I'm the boss. (*He takes up a knife.*) Now, convince me.

> *Brandon struts about like a 'boss'. Then he turns on Cod. Through most of the scene the women are mesmerized. They are watching themselves in Cod. They are silent and motionless.*

That's all very well said, young woman, 'Nothing in common,' but we have everything in common. I need you to do work and you need me to have work. We're linked, from birth until death. Star-crossed lovers igniting in the dark. (*Beat.*) Oh dear, your apron's loose. Let's just give it a little tuck. (*He runs the knife up and down Cod's body, sensually.*) You like it here, princess? (*He knocks Cod down.*) 'Where be your gibes now? Your gambols? Your songs? Your flashes of merriment?' (*Hits Cod.*) We always try to make you feel at home.

Maggot (*to Brandon, but also about her own past*) Get your fucking hands off –

Cod We have nothing to lose.

Maggot No!

Brandon What did you say? (*Hits Cod.*) I didn't quite catch that?

Maggot Don't.

Brandon You're mumbling. Girls shouldn't mumble. Nasty habit.

Roach Brandon!

Brandon Listen, young lady, I offered you that nice little office job, with a window to look out of. (*Starts to laugh.*) But you couldn't handle it. (*Hits Cod again.*) No. I mean, this little bitch couldn't even read! Can you believe it? That's what he said. That's what he said to me: this little bitch can't even read!

    Brandon raises his arm to strike Cod again but Roach's voice stops him.

Roach (*playing the 'boss' to get Brandon's attention*) Can you believe it? This little bitch can't even read! How do you sign your name then, baby, with what's left of your thumb? Can't you even defend yourself like a decent woman?

Brandon is silent. He sinks to the floor.

I didn't think so. You see, you're never gonna learn nothin', never gonna make nothin', never gonna be nothin'.

Brandon (*whispers*) I can do it. I know I can do it.

Roach You're just a piece of gut got stuck to my shoe when I walked by.

Brandon sits silent and numb. It is obvious that he is ill.

I know, Brandon. I know it better than you. 'Cause that's what they've been saying to me all my life.

Tuck enters.

Tuck What the hell's going on here? (*Sees Cod's been hit.*) Brandon's initiating the new crew again? Well, that's a 'bingo'. You're out, boy.

Cod No. Brandon was . . . He was showing me . . . How to – I slipped.

Tuck Really? (*to Brandon*) On your feet.

Brandon doesn't respond.

Roach Better get on the phone, Tuck, and call an ambulance. You got someone here who needs medical attention.

Tuck and Roach help Brandon to his feet; they lead him out.

Cod Local 226 is one of the last in the industry.

Maggot Would you shut up already?!

Cod All we have to do is fold our arms and the whole thing will stop.

Maggot You really believe that?

34

Cod Not most of the time. But it's living under water like this.

Maggot Yeah. And when you yell, it doesn't make a sound.

Cod Only bubbles.

Maggot (*shrugs*) What do you think about when you're working the meat? My hands do this thing called work, but I let my mind go somewhere else. Specially when the manager, that Baquin guy, comes to call. He likes to keep us neat, to tighten my apron when it gets loose, smooth the wrinkles down. (*Beat.*) Does that excite you? Thinking about him touching me against my will?

Cod (*puts his hand out into the air as though he were touching it*) Feel it? It's heatin' up in here.

Maggot I don't mind the heat.

Cod That's how it starts.

Maggot It's the smell I can't get used to. I've been here fifteen years. You'd think a person would get used to it.

Cod Some things a person shouldn't get used to. Myself. I was a member of K.O.L. Ever heard of them? Knights of Labour. We struck Caterpillar . . . in Peoria, Illinois . . . a couple of years ago. No. It was the McCormick Harvester Works . . . in Chicago. Quite a few years back. Four hundred thousand of us struck. Things got out of hand and the police opened fire on us. A fellow I knew, hands as big as a bear's, took a bullet in his mouth and went down right next to me.

Maggot So sometimes you're union and sometimes you're a scab?

Cod I don't always get to choose. Usually I'm union.

Maggot Not much difference anymore, union or not. Things just stay the same. Scrabblin' for something better is like scrabblin' for heaven. You only get there when you're dead.

Cod That fellow next to me was striking for an eight-hour day. For decency. Just decency.

Maggot Eight-hour day? But we've had –

Cod (*interrupts*) Ever seen a friend get shot in the mouth by a cop? It changes a person in a big way.

Maggot I suppose it would. (*Beat.*) You're sweating.

Cod It's a hundred degrees in here. Who doesn't sweat?

Maggot Maybe you're sick.

Maggot tries to touch Cod's forehead to check his temperature, but Cod jumps back, terrified at the thought of being touched.

Cod Don't. (*Beat.*) Please.

Maggot (*amused*) Did you like it that time I kissed you?

Cod I wish I could say no.

Maggot Take off your shirt. I want to see if you've got the kind of chest I like.

Cod What kind of chest is that?

Maggot I'll know it when I see it.

Cod (*turning away*) Things aren't always the way you see it.

Bell sounds and Cod and Maggot move quick to start work again.

Baquin, Tuck, Maggot and Roach in Baquin's office.

Baquin Appearances are the commodity. It's not the taste of our meat we're selling, but its appearance, its attitude. How the meat is coloured, how it shines, how it carries itself with a straight spine, even if it's boneless. (*To Tuck.*) Don't slouch. Bring me the soap and water. Good. A man won't get ahead if he slouches. But what's really getting the company image down is smudge, the smudginess of the workers. They aren't laundering their uniforms regularly.

Tuck It's tough keeping a uniform clean down there, sir.

Baquin One of your jobs is to make sure the work force looks decent. Would you say this work force looks decent? Look at the smudges, the wrinkles, the rips in the cloth.

Tuck New uniforms were due six months ago.

Baquin Nonsense. These uniforms are new. I ordered them myself. They simply haven't been cared for. We must cultivate a passion for cleanliness. The problem is that some of us simply lack passion, and passion is a clean impulse, not a dirty one. And where there is passion lacking, dirt will be lurking. (*Beat.*) Take off the uniforms, please.

Maggot and Roach look at each other in disbelief. They don't move.

My dear ladies. Those uniforms are company property and the company wants to wash its property. Right now. (*Beat.*) Take them off.

The women turn away and begin to unbutton their uniforms. Roach turns to Tuck as she undresses. He turns to leave. Baquin silently stops Maggot's hand so that she stops undressing. Until she has removed her uniform, Roach doesn't realize that she stands alone in her slip.

Just a minute, Buck. I might need your help. Give them the soap and water.

Tuck places the bucket of soap and water between the two women.

Roach I can do this in the bathroom.

Baquin This is private space here. Feel completely at home.

Tuck (*turning to leave again*) I need to check the pressure gauge on hog box number six, sir.

Baquin That can wait. Now wash.

The women don't wash.

(*shouts*) Wash!

The women take the sponges and begin to wash.

That's right. Get those smudges off. Scrub hard! Put the whiff of daintiness back in the cloth, restore that *Odiferous mundi.* That's Latin for World Odour. The smell of worldliness and cleanliness. And we do need world order, odour. (*Beat.*) Yes. Well. Don't you agree, Chuck?

The melody of this song suggests an old slave song.

Tuck (*sings*)
Every day workin' when the sun comes up
Ain't got a dime for a coffee cup.

Roach and Tuck
Work in the evenin' till the sun goes down
Listen to the singin' of the bossman's hound.

Tuck, Maggot and Roach (*sing together*)
Everyday one more dolla in my hand
Slip through my fingers like a grain a sand.*

Baquin I'm not familiar with that tune. I don't listen to top forty. I prefer classical.

Roach (*throws down her sponge*) We're finished.

Baquin (*looking Maggot over*) Yes. You are, Maggot. (*to Roach*) But you can't be. (*He takes the sponge from Maggot and gently cleans the back of her neck.*) What do you think, Maggot? Is your friend clean? (*Baquin continues sponging Maggot's neck, slowly nearing, but not quite touching, her breasts.*)

Tuck She's clean, sir.

Baquin It's hard to tell. (*He sets a chair in the centre.*) Roach, could you help us out? Please. Step up here so we can see things better?

After some moments Roach steps up on the chair.

Just as I suspected. There's dirt behind your knees.

Tuck But, sir –

Baquin Surely you can see it? Can't you, Maggot?

Maggot does not answer, but looks away from Roach.

Exactly. Well put. Smudges are attracted to the backs of knees. Finish the job.

Tuck Sir?

Baquin Scrub behind her knees.

Roach Go on, Tuck. Follow your orders.

---

*Song written in collaboration with Lisa Dixon.

Tuck kneels before Roach as she stands above him, though he doesn't wash her. She sings:

Every day one more dolla in my hand
Slip through my fingers like a grain of sand.

Baquin (*to Tuck*) Let me see your nails.

Tuck and Roach (*sing*)
One day soon dontcha know, I'll be free
Livin' in the sun so don't you worry 'bout me.

Baquin A supervisor must keep clean, short nails.

Roach and Tuck (*sing*)
O, Lord, God hear me callin', take my hand

Baquin Show me your hands.

Tuck puts his hands in his pockets.

Roach and Tuck (*sing*)
Wontcha take me, take me to the promised land.

Baquin (*shouts*) I said show me your hands!

Roach and Tuck
O, Lord, God hear me callin', take my hand
Wontcha take me, take me to the promised land.

After some moments of silence.

Baquin Well, yes. Well. Tuck. I'm ravished. I'm going to catch a bite to eat. Please have their files ready. I'd like to look them over when I get back. (*Beat.*) Would anyone like a cup of tea before they return to work?

No response from the workers, so Baquin shrugs and exits. Maggot and Roach slowly pull themselves together. Roach dresses.

Tuck It's Miss Roach, isn't it?

Roach Miss Lyles. Roach is my first name.

Tuck You taught the recorder lessons after work for employees?

Roach That was Maggot.

Tuck Could I ask where you got your name?

Roach Little girl gave it to me when I was seven. I collected bugs. The day I met her I only had a roach in my bug box. So she called me Roach. That was Maggot. Maggot calls me Roach.

Maggot exits.

Tuck That's a name that won't get you very far.

Roach It's not my name that's holding me back.

Tuck And Maggot?

Roach When I met her she looked whiter than any white kid I'd ever met. She reminded me of a maggot. The whiteness of maggots.

Tuck Yes. I can see how it came to you. White friend. That sounds like a contradiction.

Roach Sometimes it is.

Tuck Well, Roach. What do you know about snails?

Roach just looks at him.

Partula affinis. It is the last snail of its kind. This packing company is going to start a committee to raise funds for a search in the South Pacific. For a mate. I'd like you to head the steering committee. We'll call it the Salvation Nature Alliance Involving Labourers. S.N.A.I.L. Snail. (*Beat.*) The Board's hot on the idea. They've asked me to sell it.

Roach We get a new contract signed and I'll get you members for SNAIL.

Tuck You do trimming, right? Number three pay bracket? How would you like ham pumper or pickle maker?

Roach Can we speak off the record?

Tuck Of course.

Roach Last year the company tried to sell us piano lessons after work. The year before, it was ice skating for management and employees on Sunday afternoons. Free of charge. Well, let me tell you something: we're at war here. And we will not shake your hand and we will not skate with you and we will not sing Christmas carols with you for the holidays. We have nothing in common, Tuck. Nothing. And it's a sorry thing when people like you don't even have to be forced to the hook. No. Worms like you jump on the hook, take the spear right in their gut and then wriggle and say they like it. You may be a Supervisor, Tuck, but you're still a nigger and when he's through with you, you'll go out with the rest of the garbage. (*Beat.*) I'll see you there.

Tuck How about a smoker? Top pay bracket. Or a cooker? You can have your pick. (*Beat.*) It's not a colour thing anymore, Miss Roach. It's a money thing, a class thing.

Roach Yeah. It's a money thing alright and I haven't got any. But I have got a class and you, brother, are not in it. But you might be again one day. Because the colour thing never quite rubs off. You know it and I know it. And when the strings get tighter, you'll be out of a job before the maggot beside you. 'Cause you see, maggots live off of dead meat and we're the dead meat and when their bellies are full, they turn into flies . . .

Tuck (*approaching her*) And fly away?

Roach It's a way of seeing things. Sometimes it works, sometimes it doesn't.

Tuck touches her hair, briefly.

Tuck I'm sorry about the uniforms. It wasn't my idea.

Roach We've got nothing in common, Tuck. When I see you back on the kill floor, then we'll do some talking.

Tuck I heard you spit in Supervisor Burke's face when he made a go for you. Would you spit in my face?

Roach No. And you wouldn't give me a reason to, would you?

Tuck Frankly, I don't like snails myself.

Roach Don't get in our way.

SCENE TWELVE

Sausage Man appears, wandering in the empty packhouse as he speaks. Cod sits nearby, huddled in a corner, dejected and alone. The Sausage Man knows Cod is there and his words are partly a performance for Cod.

Sausage Man What happened to the dream? Our dream? I made one sausage, then two, then three. I could live off of two and sell the third as surplus. The dream as simple math. Make more than you need. Sell the excess. With a little extra cash, hire someone to make the sausages for you, while you deal with the papers and the cash. What is unjust about having another human being work for you? I employed hundreds. I gave them free trimmings. But they bit the hand that fed them. Chomp. Chomp. They did not respect the math. The math of the dream. Was there ever

43

an empire without slaves? Can there be history without
the poor? Small people die small deaths and their place in
history is the flick of a pig's tail, part of the machinery of
the living beast, but the tail end all the same. Myself, I am
an innovator. I make something from the refuse in this
world. And there will always be refuse in this world so
there will always be a place for me. It's just a time of
matter, that's all. (*He nears Cod.*) You mustn't sit on the
floor. It's damp. You'll catch a cold. (*He takes off his
jacket and puts it around Cod's shoulders.*) You should
take better care of yourself.

Cod A mollusc. In the ocean. A limpet. That's what I'd
like to be.

Sausage Man But they're so small. You might get eaten by
a seagull.

Cod Limpets live near reefs. And they have this endless,
tremendous ocean all around them but they stay their
entire lives on one rock. One rock. They never move from
that rock. And if you try to pull a limpet off its rock, it
hangs on. And the harder you pull, the more tightly it
hangs on.

Sausage Man How 'bout a walk? That'll cheer you up.

Cod I can't even imagine that kind of determination.

Sausage Man Tsk, tsk. That's not very ambitious. A
limpet? And what would you do then? Suck at a rock for
eternity?

Cod Yeah. And I'd be a part of it all. A part of the ocean.
I'd watch the tide go in and out. I'd eat algae. Digest sand.
I'd be witness to shipwrecks and sharks. The birth of an
octopus. The death of a sea cow. My mate would be a
starfish and we'd grow old together. We'd even die.
Imagine that? And millimetre by millimetre I'd travel that

single rock. And after all those years – who knows? –
maybe I'd even leave a scratch, some kind of mark on the
stone to prove I was there.

*A noise somewhere that startles Cod. He clings to the
Sausage Man, frightened.*

What? Where are we?

Sausage Man (*holding him*) Shhh. We're still here. Shhh.

Cod (*still clinging*) Where?

Sausage Man This little piggy went to market. This little
piggy stayed home. This little piggy –

Cod OK. Stop it. Stop it. (*Pulls away from the Sausage
Man.*) I know where we are. (*Looking Sausage Man over.*)
I preferred you as a Rockefeller, delving into mines,
reeking of money, not meat.

Sausage Man But you complained about the mines. Too
much coal dust in the nose. And then you caught a cough,
remember? That was a nasty cough you had.

Cod There wasn't a' one of us who wasn't sick but we
were ready to blow that mountain wide open. The fuse
was lit. But you yanked me out just before the explosion.
Just in time.

Sausage Man It might have been serious.

Cod Was it serious?

Sausage Man Nasty. Sticky. There was a mess to clean up.

Cod What's the point if I never get to see things through?
Damn you.

Sausage Man Please. Tantrums only make you hotter
quicker. My brow is cool. Come, kiss my forehead, child.

Cod turns away.

45

Without me, you'd have remained a bloody stump in your mother's belly. So ungrateful, and I your very umbilical cord . . .

Cod Then why don't you shrivel up and be gone?

Sausage Man There's a life's work in this industry. Reputations to be saved. Labour to be secured.

Cod I want something else. Anything. Forget the limpet then. Send me to an island. I'll rally the coconuts and crabs. I'll give you a good tussle. Only let me stay. In one place. Whatever the final outcome.

Sausage Man I won't risk losing you.

Cod Then I'll refuse.

Sausage Man It's your nature to resist. I can count on you. That's hard to come by in this late century. That sort of certainty. This city needs you.

Cod No. I need this city. Without you.

Sausage Man Should I sing to you again? Would that calm you?

Cod You sing like coconuts and crabs.

Sausage Man I'm sorry. (*Holds out his arm for the jacket.*) The jacket, please. It's the only one I have.

    Cod moves away.

Come now. I'm not a very convincing Mr Fisher without the threads, now am I? Do you want to be the death of me?

Cod (*sniffing the jacket*) This jacket stinks.

Sausage Man It's authentic. Mr Fisher died in it.

Cod Yeah? Well, alright then; meat this time it will be!

(*Holds up the jacket.*) And how would you like your jacket sliced, sir?

Sausage Man The sewing's a triple stitch. Take a look. Rather fine, isn't it?

Cod (*takes a knife from his pocket*) Fine did you say? One jacket, finely sliced, coming up. No fat on this one. (*He makes a neat, clean slice through the back of the jacket.*)

Sausage Man Now that's too bad.

Cod *throws the jacket at the Sausage Man's feet. The Sausage Man puts it on. The rip down the back is visible.*

Irreparable damage. No sense.

Cod I beg you.

Sausage Man You're a fighter, Cod, not a begger. Get out there and stir, spark, sputter. The labourer against my system! It's glorious. It's heroic. And we have all the time in the world. Do you know what that sounds like?

Cod I know what it tastes like. (*He spits on the floor.*) Like ashes on my tongue.

Sausage Man Listen. (*He turns his grinder. We hear a strange, sad and sensual music.*) That's the music of all the time in the world. Hear how it weeps, how it grieves and longs to be silent. But it can't. It must sing forever. Just like you. Dance to it, my child. Dance to your music.

Cod *stands transfixed as the Sausage Man turns in a circle, like a figure in a music box, dancing to the music.*

Cod in the changing room. Maggot enters. Cod has his shirt pulled up so we can see bandages around his lower back that he is just finishing retying.

Cod (*looking over his shoulder*) Ladies' changing room is across the hall.

Maggot What's the bandage for?

Cod Slipped on the kill floor. Got a steer horn in my ass. Broke three ribs. (*He begins to move away.*)

Maggot Wait. Just wait. A minute.

She approaches him. He does not turn around.

Can I touch your back?

Cod I'd rather you didn't.

Maggot Oh.

Cod It's not that I don't like you.

Maggot Save it.

Cod I'm just not the kind who sticks around.

Maggot Sure.

Cod I wouldn't want you to make a mistake.

Maggot (*meaning her hands*) I can't feel much anyway.

Cod I'm not like you think I am.

Maggot Your back is like I think you are. (*She moves close to Cod but doesn't touch him. Rather, she just stands there and feels the warmth coming from his back from a distance.*) I can feel the heat coming off your body like an August breeze. Nice. (*Beat.*) Who are you?

Cod doesn't respond.

You know, if I died, I think I'd like to lay my head down on something like you.

Cod moves away, puts on his jacket, then turns around.

Cod Who's thinking about dying?

Maggot We don't have to think about it. We're already dead.

Cod Yeah. Most of the time. But then there's that minute or two, once or twice a year. Once or twice a decade, when you think, maybe this time something is gonna change.

Maggot Nothing ever changes in Slaughter City. You just break down after so many years and they sweep you out back with the rest of the scraps. Or use you for stuffing.

Cod Whatever happened to that animal called hope?

Maggot First it got stunned, then it got slaughtered. Seems like for years I just wake and work and shit and sleep. It's a good life. Nothing to disappoint me. (*Beat.*) You know, when I was a kid there were only two things I wanted: a V8 pick-up and a boyfriend who'd let me drive. You wouldn't think that was a lot to ask for in life, would you?

SCENE FOURTEEN

Roach and Maggot at the end of the day in the changing room. Roach has her rod and lure box with her. She opens the lure box and sorts them, getting ready for the weekend.

Maggot The truth is, my uniform was cleaner than yours.

Roach Get your narrow white ass out of my face –

49

Maggot Yeah? You look like garbage. You never take your uniform home and bleach the stains out, like I do.

Roach You know what I was thinking when I stood on that chair? No. You don't know. You have no idea.

Maggot What was I supposed to do?

Roach Not one word. Didn't call my name. Didn't say, 'I'm here by your side.' Nothing.

Maggot You didn't do nothing either. Should I've let him get me like that too? Then we could've both played the dog. Oh yeah. That woulda been 'right on, sister'. (*Beat.*) I couldn't have been that kind of friend to anyone.

Roach (*examines lures while ignoring Maggot*) Ah, the rapalla. Looks like a knife in the water.

Maggot I thought I could but I guess I can't.

Roach Nickname: 'Stab in the back.' (*Holds up another lure.*) Double-headed jig. I call her 'Old two-face-strikes-again'.

Maggot I'm not making my bills.

Roach (*holds up another lure*) Big eyes: the Zephyr Puppy. Commonly known as: 'the traitor.'

Maggot I don't want to sell the truck. Could sell the tires.

Roach When you reel her in, she twitches like an insect on the water.

Maggot God damn it, I'm tired.

Roach Oh, she plays it coy. But she's got nine silver hooks, nine pretty lies just waiting for you.

Maggot You don't know what that's like. I can't even get myself off any more 'cause my hands start to shake so bad when I go into repetitive motion.

Roach Whoever named it carpal tunnel never had it. Sounds like a fish.

Maggot I was on probation last summer, remember? You piss too often, you chew your lunch too slow, your sausages aren't bent the right way. Well, I got called down to the office. My scales were off about half a point. Manager said he'd have to let me go. I said I needed the job. He said how bad. I said bad. He said show me. (*Beat.*) I showed him. (*Beat.*) Across his desk between two fern plants.

They are silent some moments.

Roach I hate ferns.

Maggot Whatever it was you wanted me to do that day, I just couldn't do it. I guess I'm not who I thought I was.

Roach That makes two of us. (*Beat.*) You know, when I was a kid I couldn't sleep at night, thinking about dying. I was so scared I'd lie in bed pinching myself awake all night so I wouldn't fall asleep because my Momma said dying was like sleeping and I didn't want to die.

Maggot Sometimes I think about dying the way I fix a bowl of cereal in the morning – I could take it or leave it.

Roach You remember Mr Morton? Our second grade teacher? You used to get jealous 'cause he would take me fishing and he wouldn't ever take you.

Maggot I remember: teacher's pet.

Roach Yeah, well, he liked fishing the way I liked it and sometimes after school he'd take me down to the stream. He was the first white man who ever treated me like a child likes to be treated. Like I had something special about me that only he could see. (*Beat.*) When Mr Morton cast a good line, his ears would go red. Red as a worm.

Maggot (*sings*)
Oh my love is like a red, red, worm.

Roach They say a worm has seven hearts and that if you
break it up in the right places, two or three of the pieces
will live. Problem was, I never knew where the hearts were
or where to put the hook in. That's why I mostly use
artificials now. (*She casts her rod as if out into the
audience and reels it back in.*) Switchback, rapalla, bass
magnet, double-headed jig. Twelve-pound line. Eight-
pound line. I was using a six-pound line that day and I
landed a four-pound small-mouth bass. You remember the
picture. That fish was longer than my arm! Almost
snapped my line. Mr Morton and I skinned it right there
and cooked it over the fire. I can tell you I was proud that
day. And Mr Morton was proud of me too. He kissed me
on the mouth four times, one kiss for each pound of that
bass. Have you ever made your teacher that proud of you?
I liked him better than my own Daddy because he took me
fishing and my own father never had time because he was
always at the packhouse splittin' hogs. (*Beat.*) Four times.
On the mouth. He said he wanted to know what my kind
. . . tasted like. (*Beat.*) That's how proud he was. That's
how. Yes. And I closed my eyes because I had to. Because
if a worm has seven hearts it could have eight and I
wanted him to know I could take it. And I took it. Right
there in the grass beside the stream. (*Beat.*) But once it's
cut you never can tell just which parts of the worm have
been killed and which parts will crawl away and start over
because all of the parts are moving. All of the parts are
trying to live. But only one or two of them do. Live.
Funny. How you can look at a body and see nothing but
the whole of it. But I know. I know which parts went on
and lived and which parts gave up and died. Can you tell
them apart? If you touch yourself, here and here? Go on.
Try it.

Maggot just watches her in silence.

Can you tell just which parts of you are dead and which parts of you are still alive? (*Beat.*) Yeah. I know what it's like, Maggot. I just don't let it lead me. And you and me are lucky. Sure-all-to-hell-lucky that we still got parts of us that are alive. (*Beat.*) All right then? When you're ready? (*Beat.*) Damn it, Maggot. I should punch you in the mouth but – (*she hands Maggot the rod and Maggot takes it*) it's the weekend and you and me are going fishing!

SCENE FIFTEEN

Cod and the Sausage Man in the empty packhouse, at night.

Cod Let me go.

Sausage Man I can't. A promise is a promise.

Cod Every promise has its crack.

Sausage Man You're becoming tiresome, Cod. Tiresome is not fun.

Cod I need to stay here. Just a bit longer.

Sausage Man I think you're in love. How sweet. How infantile. Tell me, has she seen you out of this garb?

Cod She could keep me here.

Sausage Man Ah. The strength of a woman's love to break an old promise? I like it. But you can't change the past. It's like you, condemned to repeat itself.

Cod Yeah. And I'm always at your mercy because once upon a time someone somewhere agreed that yours was the only game. But what if there were another way?

53

Sausage Man Imagine that! How exciting.

Cod What if, over time, all this friction, all this fire, began to burn a hole in your playground?

Sausage Man That's my Cod! Keep tossing that dice.

Cod Then we'd just walk through that hole to the other side. And from the stink and wreckage of your death, we'd build something new.

Sausage Man Give it your best shot!

Cod But I never get to stay around long enough to see what's left, do I?

Sausage Man Don't be sour. You're a spark for eternity. What else could you ask for?

Cod What else? What else? (*Beat.*) Just for one single moment to be without heat. To shiver. Watch my fingers turn blue. To be (*beat*) cold. Yeah. That's what I'd like. To be cold like . . . snow.

Sausage Man (*grinds his sausage machine. As he does so, it begins to snow inside the packhouse*) To be cold like snow.

Cod looks up in amazement and lifts his arms to catch the snow like a child might.

In your dreams, my friend. Only in your dreams.

Act Two

SCENE ONE

Cod and Maggot and Roach are listening to Mr Baquin, who stands in the centre of the work room, Tuck at his side. The workers all have their arms raised.

Baquin Let's try it again. Ready? And a one, two, three, go!

Baquin and Tuck do jumping jacks. The workers move their arms but they don't jump. After eight jumps or so, Tuck stops. Then Baquin stops.

Not just your arms, but your feet too. You've got to moooooove . . . You've got to moooooove. (*He clears his throat.*) Jump up and down. Like I do. You've got to learn to take care of your bodies. Your body is a temple. It belongs to God. Your body is God's property. Respect God's property. Respect God's temple with its rooms, oh, gorgeous rooms that are God's divine divisions and partitions – to gut, cut, hack, slice and stun. So jump! Leap! Exercise your gifts. Raise your bodies to the cause, make yourselves stars of motivation, co-ordination, innovation! (*Beat.*) Now. Let's try it again. And this time make an effort. And a one, two, three, go!

Everyone does jumping jacks in unison for some moments. One by one they stop. First Roach, then Maggot, then Cod, then Tuck, then Baquin.

Now take a deep breath. In, and out. In, and out. Well, I feel refreshed. How about the rest of you?

No response. The workers stare at him.

SCENE TWO

Maggot and Roach are working in the refrigeration unit among large, hanging carcasses, stamping the meat. Cod rushes in with a bucket over his head and shouts.

Cod I been robbed!

Roach and Maggot (*playing the game*) Oh my God! Tell us what happened!

Cod I been robbed by the capitalist system!

They all sing and use their tools to make music to accompany them. Cod dances about with the bucket on his head.

We stick and slit and shackle and head
We snap and trim and pull and scald
We scale and stun and scrape the meat
We pack it all for you to eat.

If there's a hell it's as hot as this
Standing all day in the blood and piss
We work in the war zone and the wages we pull
Aren't enough to keep a dog's tit full.

So fold up your arms and sit where you stand
They're gonna hear us across the land
We're sick of getting nothing but an ear of shit
This time it's enough and we say 'quit!'

Cod collapses with the bucket on his head. Brandon enters, moving slowly, like someone who has recently been ill. He steels his knife, very slowly. The others go back to work. Cod pulls loins. Brandon begins pulling loins beside Cod. Brandon watches Cod work.

Brandon Give me your knife.

Cod hands it over. Brandon examines the blade.

56

You sharpen this?

Cod Yes I did.

Brandon Manually, I see.

Cod Yes.

Brandon Good for you. But you've folded the edge over. Cutting with a knife like this you'll pull your back out. Look. It won't cut.

Brandon reaches for Cod's hand but Cod pulls back. Brandon sighs and rolls up his own sleeve and drags the blade down his arm. It doesn't cut him.

See what I mean? (*Holds the knife up between them.*) The edge of the knife is like a thin piece of hair. If you angle that steel wrong, you're going to fold the edge over.

Cod I'll work at it.

They pull loins together.

Brandon So the company won't even chat?

Maggot Sent them three proposals. They said no.

Roach And no and no.

Cod They'll bring in replacements if we strike again.

Brandon So it's 'we' now, is it? (*Beat.*) I heard about the new proposal while I was . . . out. So we've offered to cut knife time in exchange for seniority rights?

Roach We had to give them something. We're fucking tired. All of us. Almost half voted to throw in the towel. Next time we vote, it'll be over. And so will we.

Brandon We're not going to eat their contract. Ever. Isn't that what we said? (*Speaks even slower.*) See how a few . . . few . . . thousand wa . . . wa . . . watts to the brain

57

can make a fell . . . fellow . . . rea . . . rea . . . rea. . .
sonable? (*Suddenly he jumps and does a perfect cartwheel,
and ends up face to face with Roach, speaking fast, in
rhythm.*)

So. Have you made a decision
between makin' the dip
to sip the straw
or having a dip on a cone
while I sup with my cup
and smile my way up?

Maggot We didn't miss you, Brandon.

SCENE THREE

*We are back in the workroom with Cod and the Textile
Worker. It is the same dream/scene as the prelude. The
Textile Worker is the central focus but we also see
Maggot, Roach and Brandon working in silence. They are
not aware of the scene going on around them, though they
will chant with the woman.*

Textile Worker (*chants*)
Pull the cloth, punch it down, cut three out and trace.

Cod Hey! I'm talking to you!

Textile Worker
Hurry, hurry, don't go slow, keep your cheer and grace.

Cod I know you can hear me.

Textile Worker
Pull the cloth, punch it down –

Cod Look at me!

Textile Worker (*turns to look at him but looks in another* *direction, away from Cod as though she sees Cod elsewhere*) I am looking at you. I'm always looking at you.

Smoke begins to trickle in from a crack in the floor.

Cod No. No.

Textile Worker Yes. Look at your hands. They're beautiful. (*She holds up her own hands.*) Like mine once were.

Cod Get on your feet. Look what's happening.

Textile Worker Your hands are like two flames.

Cod Get up and do something!

Textile Worker All the water in the world can't put their fire out.

Cod drops to his knees and tries to cover the smoke with his hands to keep it from coming in.

Cod There's no fire. There's no smoke. Not here. So pull the cloth, punch it down.

The Sausage Man enters with his sausage machine.

All the Workers
Cut three out and trace.

Sausage Man The doors have been locked.

Textile Worker
Hurry, hurry, don't be slow –

Sausage Man From the outside.

All the Workers
Keep your cheer and grace.

Sausage Man To keep track of employees. The fire trucks are on their way. The fireman will say his ladders could only reach the seventh floor. Is this the eighth?

Cod Let us out. Open the fucking doors!

Sausage Man I don't have the key. I lost it years ago. (*Beat.*) It's already happened. You can't change it. Why upset yourself?

Cod (*turns to the other workers*) Help me with the doors. We'll break them down.

The workers go on working. They can't hear him.

You stupid bastards.

Sausage Man They can't hear you.

Textile Worker My hands sweep the cloth like water –

Cod Do you want to die?

Textile Worker (*continuing*) over the keys of a piano.

Cod Are you just going to stand there and burn?

The Sausage Man cranks his grinder and the fire increases. The workers go on working.

Sausage Man They won't ever be able to hear you. Because you're always somewhere else, my child.

Cod sinks down to the floor as in the first fire scene. At the moment he shouts the sound of the fire increases to drown out his voice.

Cod (*shouts*) Is anybody out there?

SCENE FOUR

Tuck alone on stage in Baquin's office. The chair Roach stood on still stands centre stage. He sees it. He circles it. He slowly gets undressed, then stands on the chair, as Roach did earlier. He stands still some moments, as

*though in another place and/or time. Then he gets off the
chair. He picks up his clothes. As he casually moves away,
he reaches out and tips the chair over with one finger, and
keeps walking. As it falls behind him, he looks back once.
Then exits.*

SCENE FIVE

*Cod and Brandon in the cafeteria. Brandon is seated,
engrossed in eating.*

Cod It's a scandal.

Brandon Make yourself at home. Food's not that bad.

Cod OK. Then as food it shall be.

Brandon It is food.

Cod Not always it isn't.

Brandon What is the 'it' we're talking about here?

Cod It's no longer an 'it', it's an 'isn't'.

Brandon Your ruining my lunch with your gibberish.
Can't a man have –

Cod A man should have.

Brandon – a peaceful . . . intermission? (*Returns to his
food.*)

Cod (*picking items off Brandon's plate*) Not this canned
pea, not this frozen carrot, in fact, not even this . . .

Brandon Lumpagravy.

Cod Right. Not one piece of anything comes into being
without us.

Brandon So what's new?

Cod Not even this tray. (*He takes Brandon's tray.*)

Brandon Wait a minute.

Cod What you see here is dead –

Brandon It's a pork chop.

Cod – labour. Dead labour, of past and present.

Brandon Get out of my lunch.

Cod lifts the tray and balances it between them, then swiftly slams it onto the table, face down. Brandon watches, stunned.

Cod Without the tray, the mashed potatoes slide into the cheesecake, the milk swamps the peas. This is the situation we're in today. Without the tray, and the tray being the union here, we're without a world that gives us definition and power. We're no longer a community of carrots and peas and mashed potatoes (*grabs a handful of the squashed food up in his hand*) but a handful of slops. And they'll use us to feed the hogs.

Brandon (*picks the pork chop out of the mess*) Voilà! The pork chop's the enemy, right?

Cod You got it.

Brandon What's the Big Bad Boss doing down here in the mess with the rest of us?

Cod No, no. The pork chop is the enemy in disguise. The pork chop's no better off than the peas. The pork chop's –

Brandon The scab.

Cod Bingo.

Brandon eats the pork chop.

What you see here is deregulation so that workers have no way of protecting their rights. When we make a stink 'cause we're offered part-time jobs with twelve-hour shifts, big business just ups and moves over the border or across the sea. It's the sort of unsavoury wage situation you see here when your milk and gravy meet the cheesecake and it begins to dissolve.

Brandon If we were having jello it wouldn't have made a whole lot of difference.

Cod There's always room for jello because we're one of the only industrialized nations where illegal firings and the hiring of scabs are common practice.

Brandon Those fucking pork chops.

Cod hands Brandon a fork and Cod takes a spoon.

Cod We're back to the depression. Eat. No. Back to the Victorian age. (*He eats from the table.*) Robber Barons are again free to trade – eat! – over our dying bodies. Everything and nothing has changed.

Brandon, to his own surprise, eats from the mess as well.

But guess what? (*Pounds on the food with fork.*) No matter how many times they pull the tray out from under us, smash, mash and pulverize our communities – (*takes another bite*) we're still here.

Brandon And we're still eating.

Cod Right. (*Beat.*) You have the cheesecake. (*Looking the food over.*) If you can find it.

Cod and Maggot are on break. Cod is checking over his belt tools.

Maggot A 1965 baby-blue F100 Ford, long bed, with a V8 so hot I can blow the pants off the highway in third gear.

Cod Must be some truck.

Maggot Yeah. Only it's sitting in my yard right now with a main seal leak and bad mounts. I'm doing the bus these days. You a compact man?

Cod I know a good truck.

Maggot Well, you don't know my truck. I'm the only one who can drive it 'cause it's three-on-a-tree and it sticks in second.

Cod Fords are temperamental.

Maggot Yeah. The engine sweats, foams just a little at the edges. The trick isn't in your hand, really; it's in your groin. You got to rock your hips at just the right rhythm to lubricate the hitch on that second gear.

Cod I could drive a truck like that.

Maggot Ever changed gears with your mouth? Not too tight and when the pressure's right and just about to blow, you open it up, wide, and shoot across that highway with the windshield shattering over your head like snow and the sun pouring down your throat like water. And there's no turning back.

Cod Ford, huh? A person could go to hell for driving a Ford. They'll put a stick shift up your ass and the Devil will cruise you all over his island singing 'Ford-gives-you-better-ideas'. All through eternity.

Maggot Should have figured you were Chevy.

Cod A '58, V8, short bed with chrome hubs, AM radio, four on the floor and no hitch. But not everyone can drive a Chevy. You got to have the proper wrist action or you'll burn the gears. And if your hands are dry (*spits in palm*) you won't get the grip you need. (*Takes out a screwdriver or other sharp work tool.*) You drive a Ford soft but a Chevy's got to be treated rough. It's what a Chevy likes, 'cause it's an immoral engine and it can take it. Slap it some gas in first and when you have the speed up and the friction between the rubber and the road is sending sparks down your spine (*sticks the screwdriver into the ground or box between Maggot's legs. This should be done suddenly and would frighten anyone but Maggot. Cod takes hold of the screwdriver as though it were a stick shift between Maggot's legs*) then fast into second, straight on and hard. (*Moves stick into second.*) Now third's a risk. Third is going down on the engine. But you got to keep up the speed. And speed isn't a motion, it's a texture. And it's not dry. No. Speed is wet. Speed is an ocean, and third's a deep gear, a diver's gear, only for the brave at heart gear, and I open up the vents 'cause my cylinders need some air, and then down, down, (*moves stick into third, closer to Maggot's crotch*) and lock into third.

Some moments of silence.

Maggot And what about the last one: fourth gear?

Cod unsticks the screwdriver and turns away to finish checking his tool belt.

Hey! What about fourth gear?

Cod I never tell a girl how to get into fourth gear. She's got to find that out herself. I will tell you it's not about breaking the sound barrier. It's about breaking light, just like breaking ice under your wheels.

Maggot Never met anyone like you.

Cod I'm not surprised. Want to see a trick? (*He touches the floor/ground with his fingers and where he touches it, it begins to smoke.*)

Maggot Aren't we the boy scout.

Cod With some women it works.

Maggot Son of a bitch.

Cod Don't think so. I never knew my mother. She died in the fire at . . . the . . . Triangle Shirtwaist Company . . . in New York City, some time ago. Turn of the century.

Maggot Just when were you born?

Cod The fire started in a rag bin on the seventh floor, swept through the eighth, ninth and tenth floors. Mostly young women. They burned to death at their work tables. My mother jumped. A lot of them did. They went in pairs. Holding hands. Nothing below them but concrete. My mother landed on top of some others. She wasn't crushed up like the rest of them. I was inside her. She was dead but I wasn't. When the doctors found out I was in there, they ventilated her for five months. It was an experiment. They'd already filled out her death certificate. Then they cut her open and took me out.

Maggot I heard about that fire.

Cod Yeah. I was born from a dead woman.

Maggot That fire happened over eighty years ago.

Cod It's a hard way to come into the world.

Brandon sneaks into the women's changing room. He's not sure what he's looking for. He sees a woman's work dress. He smells and touches it.

Brandon 'I have lain in prison . . . Out of my nature has come wild despair . . .

He takes the dress in his arms. Roach enters, watches unobserved for some moments.

. . . an abandonment to grief that was piteous even to look at.' (*Beat.*) No. Not on your knees. (*He tries again.*) My darling, my dreams are dark, dark, dark. (*Beat.*) Damn. Don't bring up colour. (*He tries again.*) When I am with you I feel the . . . the shadows of our desire floating and . . . light, no . . . floating and . . . luminous above us, delirious with . . . with . . . intercourse. Intercourse? Shit. (*Beat.*) Can I hold your hand?

Roach (*appears*) Now I like this show better than the last one, cherub. But you could use some lessons. (*Beat.*) Put the dress on.

They watch each other some moments.

I mean it.

Brandon glances quickly over his shoulder to make sure they're alone.

Brandon Please, sir. Avert your eyes. (*He takes off his clothes, turning away to do so.*) No peeking!

Roach watches him undress and put the dress on as he speaks the following.

Oh, I'm just a girl, a waif like a wafer you could snap in two, just a gosling in distress, an egret with no inlet to satisfy my pitiable appetites.

Roach Shush up, baby doll. Or I'll tear your fucking heart out with my teeth.

Brandon Oh no, no, no. (*Beat.*) Oh yes, yes, yes.

Roach is silent.

Well, go on you brute. Tear me into tiny, little pieces.

Roach I forget the script.

Brandon Now you force me.

Roach I force you.

Brandon Yeah. (*Beat.*) Please, please, pretty please.

Roach (*approaches Brandon and takes hold of the collar of the dress*) Isn't this the part where I . . .

Brandon Exactly.

Roach And I do it all the way down . . .

Brandon You got it.

Roach I won't be able to wear it again if I do that.

Brandon Don't worry, darling. I've got one at home I can lend you . . .

Roach Shut up.

Roach rips the dress open so that Brandon's chest is exposed. This should be done how we've seen it in countless melodramatic films.

I could get into this style.

Brandon And now you . . . go on . . . now you . . .

Roach Chew your mouth up, right?

Brandon And the eternal flames of hell engulf us.

Roach I don't think so.

Brandon Trespass matures the soul.

Roach It wouldn't be a game out there, Brandon.

Brandon This is the nineties.

Roach A Puerto Rican friend of mine had some teeth kicked out for dating a white girl.

Brandon My friends won't mind; I don't have any.

Roach What's the deal? Does it make you feel *bad* 'cause I'm black?

Brandon You want me.

Roach You're a boy, Brandon.

Brandon You want me and you hate me for it.

Roach This is a kid's game. I'm not playing.

Brandon You're a coward.

Roach I just like things simple.

Brandon Look. These are the facts. I like your mouth. It's the only place on earth I ever felt like laying a foundation to make a home.

Roach This wouldn't be simple.

Brandon I have this dream sometimes. And in the dream the scars on my mouth are gone and my mouth is . . . like it's . . . scorched, seared, and then you kiss me and your kiss is so cold. (*He gently runs a finger over her lips.*) Like an apple in the snow.

Roach removes Brandon's hand.

When I wake up from that kiss, my pillow is always wet and I'm crying like a baby.

Roach A kiss is a dangerous thing.

Brandon It's a dangerous thing to live without it. (*Beat.*) Are you afraid of me?

Roach (*laughs*) I'm afraid of me.

Brandon I won't give it up.

Roach No. I don't think you will. All right. (*She takes one of Brandon's knives.*) I'll give you a kiss. If.

Brandon If?

Roach If you can take this knife from me. (*Beat.*) But if either one of us bleeds, if either one of us gets so much as a paper cut, it's over. And we'll never talk about us again. Agreed? (*Beat.*) Agreed?

Brandon Yeah. Completely.

Roach puts the blade between her teeth. Slowly and carefully she passes the knife from her mouth to Brandon's mouth. In doing this, they are also in a 'kiss'. During this transfer, Brandon is pushed to his knees. He now holds the knife between his teeth as he kneels.

Roach That's where I like my Tarzan. On his knees.

SCENE EIGHT

Maggot and Roach on break. Roach drinks a glass of water. They hardly hear what the other is saying.

Maggot I've been thinking about trading the Ford.

Roach He's a kid. But he's a smart kid.

Maggot You ever had a Chevy?

Roach He's not really a kid, I mean he's twenty-two. That's about . . . (*She counts on her fingers.*)

Maggot A Chevy can take a lot of rust.

Roach Not so bad.

Maggot And the front end won't go out at a hundred thousand.

Roach But he's awfully white. Don't you think he's awfully white?

Maggot He's Irish. They don't get much sun.

Roach A bit young and a bit white.

Maggot How much older are you, about a decade?

Roach Thanks.

They laugh, then sit in silence some moments.

Maggot I love you, you know.

Roach What's out there will keep coming between you and me. If you ever forget it, we're finished. When it comes down to it, they're going to try and break one of us, and more likely than not, it's going to be me. And you're going to stand by and watch.

Maggot I couldn't get a job anywhere else.

Roach You couldn't get a friend like me anywhere else.

Maggot That's for sure.

Roach So has he got a spotty ass?

Maggot I haven't got that close yet. (*Beat.*) I've had some crushes, you know, pretty serious before. But I never felt like the ones I knew could reach down inside me, grab a hold of my tail bone and turn me inside out, like a shirt.

Roach I know what you mean.

Maggot And Cod's got this smell . . . Ahhh . . . A smell

71

like . . . something that's just about to burn.

Roach I kissed Brandon the other day.

Maggot No!

Roach It was . . . interesting.

Maggot Interesting? What's he taste like?

Roach Like nothing. (*Beat.*) Nice.

Maggot This one's over my head.

Roach Yeah. It is. (*Beat.*) Close your eyes.

    Maggot does. Roach tilts Maggot's face up.

Brandon tastes . . . (*She pours the water slowly and gently onto Maggot's face.*) like this. Like water. Like drinking one, two, three glasses of water.

SCENE NINE

Roach, Cod and Maggot are working in the shadows. The Sausage Man appears. No one sees him but Cod.

Sausage Man Pull the cloth, punch it down, cut three out and trace. (*Beat.*) It's time for you to go.

Cod Not yet.

Sausage Man I can feel the heat coming off your body a hundred years from now. Why don't we go there?

Cod No.

Sausage Man You're trying my patience.

Cod Hey, all of you. Look at this son of a bitch?

Sausage Man I've let you stay far too long already.

Cod Check this joker out!

The workers go on working.

Sausage Man Listen. I'm getting tired of playing opposites.

Cod Go back to the hell you crawled out of.

Sausage Man I want you to come work for me. On my side this time. We'd make a good team. You're sensitive. You listen to the meat. You'd know how to coax it into my grinder without a struggle. Without a strike. We could start anew.

Cod This time it's going to be different.

The Sausage Man laughs at Cod. Cod turns away from Sausage Man.

I can't touch her. I can't. You know that. I can't touch anyone like that. I'd burn them to a cinder. Turn their heart to a chunk of coal. But in my head. No. That you can't stop. In my head I touch her over and over. Again and again. And her skin is cold and sweet. Ice forms at the corners of her mouth. Just before we kiss. And across the world it's winter. In the fields. Inside the houses. Even under our tongues. Winter. (*Beat.*) But even in my own head, I can't make her touch me. Because I don't know what it's like to be touched. What? What? Does it cut or maul? Scratch or tear? Tell me. Is it pain? You don't know. But it must be pain, because my heart is a cheap toy and it breaks inside my chest each time I try to imagine: what would it feel like to have a hand that's not my own touch me? To have her hand on my breast? Her fingers along my spine. Her hard mouth against my hip. Across my thighs. And what would it be like to stop moving at that touch? To stand still and listen? Just listen. To the pulse in her wrist. No rage, no hurry, no you and me, no struggle. Just her blood, to and fro, in her wrist, against my ear. (*Beat.*) I am alone. I have never been anything but alone. Let her touch me. And I'll know where I am.

Sausage Man What a sermonizer the decades have made you. You'd've made your mother proud. But reality won't be changed, Cod.

Cod It's nothing more than a bucket of clay, and this time we're going to shape it.

Sausage Man It might go bad if you push it. Things aren't ripe yet.

Cod Yeah, well sometimes history's just not ready for you and so you give it a shove.

Sausage Man Snap of my fingers and you're toad's dust.

Cod But then there's no conflict. And if there's no conflict, then I won't exist. And neither will you. (*Beat.*) You can send me anywhere, but you can't make me do what you want. I quit.

Sausage Man Damn you. Damn you! (*Beat.*) All right. If you won't play, then you'll have to pay. But how much?

He gestures to the shadows, where in the darkness we see the shadow of the Textile Woman working. She shines with a strange light.

How much will you pay? (*Beat.*) Listen. Can you hear her? She's talking. Oh yes, and laughing. Because it's Friday and it's almost time to quit work.

Cod puts his hands over his ears so he won't hear Sausage Man, who seems to be physically hurting him by recounting the story.

And she feels you kick inside her and she whispers

74

something to you and she is happy because she's managed to borrow a crib from a friend and because the woman sitting across from her is telling a joke about Jack be nimble, Jack be quick, Jack tripped over the candle stick. Stupid, stupid Jack. Now flames are coming up through the floorboards at her feet. Can you hear her, Cod? She's not laughing anymore. No. She's making another sound now. Listen.

We hear the sound of pressure being released, the sound of something bursting forth from its restraints. Then we hear a scream of pain from off-stage. At the moment of the scream, Cod shouts.

Cod No!

All of the workers look in the direction of the scream and freeze.

SCENE TEN

Brandon is lying on the floor. Roach and Cod are beside him. Maggot paces.

Maggot Ten minutes. They said ten minutes.

Roach Where's the fucking first aid! He's not breathing.

Cod (*to Maggot*) Call the fire department.

Roach He's not breathing!

Cod Tell them we got an ammonia line break at hog box number six.

Maggot exits.

Roach That's it, Brandon. Breathe. Breathe. Slow. Breathe slow.

Brandon's lungs make a terrible sound as he tries to breathe.

Cod (*shouts to off-stage*) Maggot? Get him some water. Maggot?

Brandon tries to speak but can't.

Roach Shhhh. Just breathe.

Brandon (*begins to struggle*) Fuck.

Cod (*shouts*) Maggot?! (*to Roach*) Keep his head back. (*Takes out a knife and rips open Brandon's shirt.*)

Roach What the hell are you doing?

Cod His windpipe's gone. I'm punching a hole so he can get some air. (*He cuts into Brandon's neck to make a hole so he can breathe. This is a medical procedure and Cod knows what he's doing.*)

Roach Where are they?

Cod Keep his head back.

Roach Maggot!

Cod strips off his shirt to put it under Brandon's head.

Cod It will help him breathe.

Cod has chest wraps underneath to hold down her breasts. Cod is a woman. Brandon tries again to speak.

Roach Shut up. Don't talk.

Maggot enters. She sees Cod.

Maggot Jesus Christ.

Cod Have they shut down the mains?

Roach Ssshhhhh.

Maggot I don't know.

Roach (*kisses Brandon, gently, on the mouth*) Stay with us.

> *Sausage Man slowly walks across the stage. Only Cod sees him. Sausage Man kneels beside Brandon and gently blows into Brandon's neck, as though blowing out a candle. Brandon is dead.*

SCENE ELEVEN

Baquin in his office. Supervisor Tuck paces back and forth.

Tuck Damage is at a minimum. They were able to shut down the mains within minutes.

Baquin He should have been wearing safety equipment.

Tuck We don't have any.

Baquin Nonsense. I filled out an order.

Tuck We've got no sprinkler system, most of the extinguishers are shot.

Baquin That wasn't his job.

Tuck Half the safety exit doors are bolted shut.

Baquin The boy was out of line.

Tuck He had the assignment.

Baquin Call the insurance company. I want them to know that he wasn't wearing the required safety equipment.

Tuck We don't have any safety equipment.

Baquin He was careless.

Tuck I changed three of those gauges myself two days ago. That ammonia is so cold in a liquid form and it touches you and it's like taking a lit match –

Baquin The board is breathing down my neck.

Tuck – tttssshhh – it will burn you that quick.

Baquin Just make sure the papers know why it happened.

Tuck Mr Baquin. (*Beat.*) That's what it does in a vapour form in your lungs.

Baquin I don't appreciate your (*beat*) tone in this time of crisis. You've done well considering your . . . your beginnings. Your fellows wallow in blood and muck, Buck. You've been given a chance –

Tuck I earned –

Baquin You earned? You've worked at opportunities offered by this company. The bottom line here, boy, is – (*holds out his hands to Tuck*) don't bite the hands that feed you.

Tuck (*looks at Baquin's extended hands. Then his own*) See these hands?

Baquin Look clean enough to –

Tuck (*interrupts*) Oh, they're clean enough. So clean I can't even see them anymore. I used to have hands. Good, strong, black hands that did what I told them to do. They were smart and skilful, good at whatever job I asked them to do. That didn't mean they still didn't complain and ache and bruise and bleed. They very near went for broke at some jobs. But they were mine and they had a knowledge, a vocation, and when I went home at the end of the day, my hands went with me, and sometimes they played and strayed – strayed to other hands, caressed other hands, along and down and in between –

Baquin Just what the hell do you –

Tuck (*interrupts*) Now I got this almighty position. Promotion: but no hands may apply. You know what my hands do now? They hold a clipboard, or they hang at my side. And at the end of the day when I go home, I go home without them. (*Beat.*) A man without hands. What do you think, Mr Baquin? On pay day, how do you think he counts his change?

Baquin is at a loss to answer Tuck. He stares at him for some uncomfortable moments.

Baquin I see. Yes. Well. I'm sorry. Now listen to me closely: if the papers pick up on that . . . that Cod character. Christ. This industry is bringing in the likes of him. Fire him. Her. Whatever.

Tuck Cod can do the work of two men on the kill floor.

Baquin A person like that shouldn't be handling meat. If the public gets a hold of this. It's unsanitary. It's unnatural.

Tuck What's unnatural is that we figured she was a man so we started her off at the top. If we'd known she was a woman –

Baquin (*interrupts*) What are you saying? You've got to learn to articulate –

Tuck (*interrupts*) But what's really unnatural, Mr Baquin, is for a twenty-two year old boy to have his lungs burned out of his chest.

Baquin A man like you needs to speak clearly, to have command –

Tuck I changed three of those lines myself. It could've been me instead of him.

Baquin Nonsense. You would have been wearing our safety equipment.

Tuck That's the truth of it. It could've been anybody in this fucking packhouse. Anybody but you 'cause you don't change lines. No. You'll never change lines.

Suddenly Tuck picks up the bowl with the snail in it and smashes it to the ground. They look at the broken glass between them.

SCENE TWELVE

Maggot and Roach wait for Cod. She enters dressed as usual, only without her work jacket. She is carrying heavy chains with which they plan to chain the doors.

Cod We could take this place over *after* the funeral.

Roach No. We do it now. Before they get wind of it and lock us out.

Maggot I figured the next time we saw you it would be in a skirt.

Cod A girl can't chase a steer if she's wearing a skirt.

Maggot A girl can't chase a man if she's wearing a jockstrap.

Cod I don't wear a jockstrap.

Maggot Well, thank God for that.

Cod Except when I go out on the town and want to make the effort.

Roach You are one confused girl.

Cod I've never been more certain.

Maggot Get this, Roach: she was born from a corpse.

Cod I was born from a fire.

Maggot (*picks up one of the knives*) You've been lying to us all this time. Pretending you were what you're not.

Cod You're the one who pretended.

Roach What's the matter, Maggot? She's got the same ass you were mooning about.

Maggot (*holds the knife to Cod's cheek*) So are you a bastard or a bitch?

Cod Depends on the job.

Sausage Man appears elsewhere on stage.

Maggot You think you're something special?

Maggot makes a small cut on Cod's cheek. Cod doesn't flinch.

You bleed like the rest of us. (*Throws the knife down.*) That's for not thinking you could trust us.

Cod It wasn't a matter of trust.

Maggot No, it was a matter of money.

Cod And a matter of balls. Working like a man, I feel more like a gal. Know what I mean?

Roach We've got eight minutes 'til we take over and lock ourselves in.

Maggot Which changing room are you gonna use?

Roach Anybody that wants out better go now.

Cod Want to see a trick?

Maggot I've seen enough.

Cod No you haven't. It's just beginning. (*Holds out her hand.*) Go on. Touch me.

> *Maggot touches Cod's hand and then pulls back as though burned.*

Sausage Man I think it's time I took things back in hand. (*Exits.*)

Roach We got three minutes 'til we lock the doors. Help me with the chains!

> *Other workers and Roach lay out the heavy chains.*

Maggot (*to Cod*) Have you got the guts of a woman or a man?

Cod I've got guts. Years of them. More than enough for both of us.

Maggot Then I dare you: take off your shirt.

Cod Really? What do I get in return?

Maggot Name it.

Cod You knew what I was.

Roach (*still laying out chains to lock the doors with*) Let's get on with it.

Maggot I want to see if you've got the kind of chest I like.

Cod And what kind is that?

Roach One minute to lock.

Maggot I'll know it when I see it.

> *Cod strips off her shirt. She is still wearing the bandage.*

Roach Forty-five seconds.

Cod Things aren't always the way you see it.

Roach Thank God for that.

Cod All right. You can look, but don't touch.

Maggot What if I want to?

Cod You could get burned.

Roach Thirty seconds.

Maggot That's what I want.

Cod unwinds a piece of the bandage and hands it to Maggot who begins to circle Cod, unwinding the bandage as Roach counts down.

Roach Ten, nine, eight, seven –

Maggot six, five, four –

Roach and Maggot three, two, one.

The bandage is unrolled and drops to the floor. Maggot can see Cod's chest.

Maggot and Roach Lock.

Maggot and Cod kiss. At the moment of the kiss we hear the very loud sound of heavy doors being pulled shut and locking, echoes of many doors locking and locking. Then silence.

SCENE THIRTEEN

Baquin is alone and talking to himself.

Baquin Tuck. You're a good man. I want you to go in there, right now, and check on our workers. Let me know what their moooooooooo. Their moooooooooooo. (*He stops speaking and begins to chew his cud much as a cow would.*) Oh Tuck. My dear Tuck. Come back to me. You can't leave. Please, please, come back. It's lonely in here. The ultimate loneliness. Imagine: to be the last of your kind.

Sausage Man enters. Baquin is startled. Sausage Man carries a large net with him which he hides behind his back.

You're not Tuck.

Sausage Man You're not happy making my sausages anymore.

Baquin Oh yes I am.

Sausage Man No. You aren't. This is a terrible disappointment. Production has all but stopped. You see? (*He cranks his sausage machine.*) It's empty. I've run out of bits and pieces. No bits and pieces, no sausages.

Baquin How can I help you?

Sausage Man Get those doors open so we can move in there and crank things up again.

Baquin It's out of my hands.

Sausage Man nears Baquin, who becomes nervous. Sausage Man steps on something, then looks at the bottom of his shoe.

What's the matter?

Sausage Man Looks like a bit of snot got stuck to my shoe.

Baquin Oh no, oh no.

Sausage Man It's time for a little intervention.

Baquin The eternal night of extinction.

Sausage Man Why, they've frightened you, haven't they?

Baquin Nonsense. This strike is illegal. I'll call out the National Guard. (*Calls.*) Tuck! Get in here. Tuck!

Sausage Man Shhhh. I can see it's time. Time for some new blood. Would you like some grass? (*He pulls some grass from his pockets and holds it out to Baquin.*)

Baquin It's not my fault. That mob in there are tearing me limb from limb. They're cutting me to pieces. They're frying my bacon. The whole industry is being grilled to hell.

Sausage Man It's fresh grass. I picked it myself.

Baquin sniffs the grass. Suddenly he chomps at it, chews hungrily.

That's it. That's it. Yes. They've been cutting you to pieces. I can see that. Into little tiny pieces that are so small no one will have any use for them. No one but me.

Baquin Stay away from me.

Sausage Man I can turn you into something useful.

Baquin No thank you. I'm not in the mooooooooooooooooooooooooooo.

He clears his throat but nothing else will come out but the sounds of a cow. He begins to chew his cud again. Sausage Man raises his net and moves in on Baquin.

Mooooooooooooooooo?

Baquin's 'moo' is cut short when the net descends over his head.

Upstage, the workers stand in a circle around Roach. The workers have their backs to the public. All the cast should be used in this scene as workers.

Roach My friends. Welcome to Slaughter City. This is a place where things go and go and go. Now this is a place where things stop. Machinery stops. Cows stop. Pigs stop. We stop. And most importantly, the profits stop. And whenever the profits stop, things heat up fast. From now on, anything can happen. And we're going to have to be ready for it.

Roach and the workers now freeze in their scene as Cod enters from one side of the stage and the Sausage Man enters from the opposite side. Baquin's tie hangs from his grinder.

Sausage Man (*puts his grinder down in front of him, centre stage*) I've been thinking it over. You're right. Why play by the old rules? This might turn out to be the gamble we've been waiting for. The two of us here, together. At last. But will both of us be here to mop up the mess? (*He laughs with true delight.*) What a gamble! What a risk! I feel like my old self again. As you said, sometimes history just isn't ready for you so you give it – (*He lights a match.*) a shove.

The Sausage Man drops the match into the top of the grinder and it makes a small flame. Cod stands watching, transfixed. She speaks as though in a trance.

Cod I'm with the Knights of Labour . . . No . . . With the United Mine . . . (*She shakes her head, trying to locate herself.*) No. I know where I am.

Sausage Man laughs.

Sausage Man (*sings*)
'Oh where, oh where can my little dog be?'

Cod I'm in a chicken processing plant. Somewhere in the broiler belt, in 1891 . . . No. It was 1991 . . . A long time ago. Decades and decades from now.

Sausage Man They died on the assembly line.

Cod Yes. That was in . . . Hamlet. In . . . South . . . in North Carolina.

Sausage Man The chickens burned.

Cod The doors were chained shut. From the outside.

Sausage Man Cluck. Cluck. Cluck. Mooooooooooooo.

Cod That was at the Triangle Shirt Waist Company . . . A whole century from now. On the seventh . . . No! The chains were on the outside . . . No, no . . . The chains are on the inside. And this is somewhere else!

Sausage Man This is nowhere else. And there was a fire.

Cod Yes. There was a fire.

Sausage Man See you on the other side? *Bon voyage*, my friend.

Split scene: the Textile Worker is standing on the window ledge. She is dressed in a long, flowing dress from a time even before her time. A strange light lights her. She looks radiant. The Sausage Man appears beside her. Cod continues to try and locate herself. She is not consciously aware of the Textile Worker.

Cod There was a fire.

Textile Worker It started in a rag bin.

Cod On the seventh floor.

Sausage Man The workers burned.

Cod Yes. (*Beat.*) No!

Textile Worker And this is the eighth floor. I'm standing at the open window and the heat is so big behind me that it's melting the dress off my back. My hair starts to burn. I know I'm going to jump. That way I'll have a few more seconds. Alive. (*Words overlapping slightly with Cod's.*) And I want –

Textile Worker/Cod – a few more seconds.

Textile Worker Women are jumping out of the windows around me and below me, on the lower floors. From up here, they look like handkerchiefs falling to the ground.

Sausage Man (*making the sounds of a fire truck*) Ding, ding, ding.

Cod (*seemingly splitting between the past and the present moment. As before, she seems to be physically affected by what is happening around her*) Yes. The fire trucks. In the distance.

Textile Worker The ledge I'm standing on has started to burn under my feet. The soles of my shoes are gone. (*Beat.*) I lean to jump, holding my belly where my four-month-old child is still alive within me, for a few seconds more. And then he's there and he tells me –

Sausage Man I can save your child.

Cod No!

Textile Worker And I say yes, yes, and I make the promise –

They chant the 'promise'.

Sausage Man 'If the child is my spark –

Textile Worker/Cod (*slightly overlapping*) – forever and ever –

Sausage Man – to light up the dark –

Textile Worker/Cod – withersoever –

Sausage Man – I choose to send her –

Textile Worker/Sausage Man (*chant together*) – she'll live.'

Textile Worker And I agree to everything. Because I know her already. Because I want her to live.

Cod There was a fire.

Textile Worker And then I jump.

Sausage Man (*angry now*) The workers burned!

Cod No! This is now. Not the day after. This is this hour.

Textile Worker And in those seconds with the wind rushing by me, tearing my dress from my body, I remember only one thing, being asked once, as a child: 'If you had five seconds left to live –

Cod This hour.

Textile Worker – what would you do?'

Cod I'm not going to leave.

Textile Worker I didn't answer the question because as a child I didn't know.

Cod We have to do something . . . We have to . . . Yes.

Textile Worker But I know now. And so I do it.

Cod Because this is right now.

Textile Worker I laugh.

Cod And it's . . . right here in front of . . .

Textile Worker I laugh because I feel her move inside me like a flame. (*She opens her arms as if to jump.*) I laugh because I know she will never die.

> *Cod has located herself. She turns to the workers who all have their backs to her and she shouts out, as though she were already somewhere else, as though her voice is crossing a great distance of time and place between herself and her fellow workers.*

Cod Fire!

> *For a moment no one moves and we hear the sound of flames and burning. Then all the workers suddenly hear Cod's warning and one after another the workers turn sharply around, in quick succession and this time, before it's too late, they all see the fire and move towards it to put it out. The fire roars up brightly a moment in front of them, and then goes out at the same time that there is a blackout.*

Bibliography

Barrett, J. R. *Work and Community in the Jungle: Chicago's Packinghouse Workers, 1894–1922.* University of Illinois Press, 1990.

Castle, T. *The Apparitional Lesbian: Female Homosexuality and Modern Culture.* Columbia University Press, 1993.

Churchill, W. and Vander Wall, J. *Agents of Repression: The FBI's Secret War Against the Black Panther Party and the American Indian Movement.* South End Press, 1990.

Engels, F. and Marx, K. *Manifesto of the Communist Party.* International Publishers, New York, 1983.

McGrath, T. *Selected Poems, 1938–1988.* Copper Canyon Press, 1988.

Rachleff, P. *Hard-Pressed in the Heartland: The Hormel Strike and the Future of the Labor Movement.* South End Press, 1993.

Roediger, D. R. *The Wages of Whiteness: Race and the Making of the American Working Class.* Verso, 1993.

Sinclair, U. *The Jungle.* Penguin Classics, 1985.

Stromquist, S. *Solidarity and Survival: An Oral History of Iowa Labor in the Twentieth Century.* University of Iowa Press, Iowa City, 1993.

Williams, R. *Modern Tragedy: Essays on the Idea of Tragedy in Life and in the Drama.* Stanford University Press, 1966.

Yates, M. D. *Longer Hours, Fewer Jobs: Employment and Unemployment in the United States.* Monthly Review Press, New York, 1994.